SEVEN

Secrets of the Rainbow

The Journey Begins

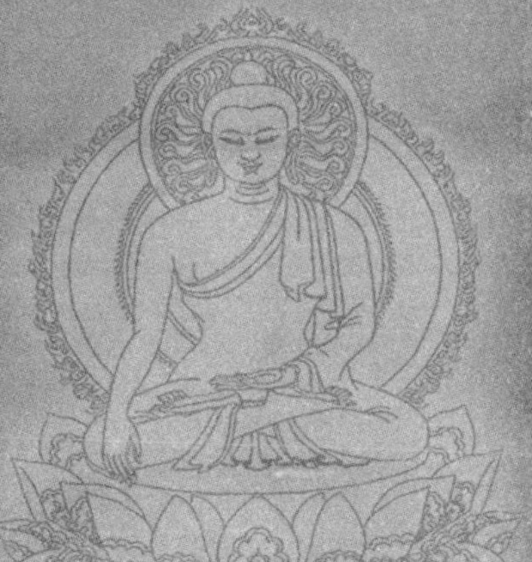

Abhilash Bhattacharya

All rights reserved; no part of this publication may be reproduced or transmitted by any means, electronic, mechanical, photocopying or otherwise, without the prior written permission of the publisher.

Published by
Sanskriti Prakashan
37/002, Sanskruti, Thakur Complex,
Kandivali(east), Mumbai - 400101.
Tel: 022-28547734/35

Copyright © Abhilash Bhattacharya 2010
Cover illustrations copyright © Abhilash Bhattacharya 2010
Cover designed by Ritika Jhunjhunwala

SEVEN SECRETS OF THE RAINBOW
The Journey Begins
ISBN 978-81-909414-0-2

Printed by
Snehesh Printers
320A, Shah & Nahar Ind. Est. A-1,
Lower Parel, Mumbai-400013.

To Shaheb Dadu, my grand father,
who has had an indelible impression on my life.

Acknowledgement

Someone asked me to describe my feelings after completing my first novel. I expressed it in one word: gratitude.

I am eternally grateful to God for blessing me with this wondrous experience of human life.

How do I thank Baba and Ma, my beloved parents who gave me not only this beautiful gift of Life, but also the gift to dream big and realise it. I am what I am because of the foundation they laid for me, with love and care.

My childhood has shaped my existence. An integral part of my childhood have been my sister, Krishna and my brother, Ajoy. They have been with me through thick and thin.

Life offers challenges to all of us. I had my share. The one person who stood by me in every situation, who prodded me along to complete this novel, against all odds, is my dear wife. Thank you, Mona.

In these times of audio-visual media attack, the habit of reading is dying off. There is lack of good literature for children in our country. I remember how incomplete I used to feel when I had to tell the same old bed time stories to my son Kumar, when he was younger. In a way, this novel is an outcome of that shortcoming. Kumar is a teenager now. Thank God that I completed this novel before he would grow up to say, "What is this childish stuff you have written, Baba?" And I would have had to say, "Wait until you get married and have kids, Beta!"

This novel could not be complete without the support of some of my very caring colleagues. I am indeed grateful to Rahela for carefully editing my novel, to Madonna for painstakingly typing it, to Ritika for her beautiful cover design and to Dinesh, Disha and Kumar for efficiently helping me market it. My sincere thanks to my good friend Tanuja Chandra for her valuable advice. I am reminded of the support of my uncle and aunt Arun and Purobi Bhattacharya in promoting my work. My humble thanks to them. My readers may find this strange but my heart is filled with affection for the unconditional love and support given to me by my pet Sheena, who unfailingly sat beside me sharing every single moment of writing this novel.

Two great people who turned around my life and gave a meaning to it are revered Shri Devidas Hirode and dear Prasad Karmarkar. I shall be ever so grateful to them.

My personal and professional life has been touched by so many wonderful people, great books, and memorable films that have helped me reach where I am today. Though I may not be able to remember and recount every one of them individually, I would like to thank each one of them most sincerely for supporting me in their own way to complete my most prized possession, this novel: 'SEVEN – Secrets of the Rainbow.'

Any creative writing is of no use unless someone picks it up and reads it. I thank all my readers for finding my novel worthy of reading.

*

CONTENTS

1. A JOURNEY BEGINS 1
2. SHOCK OF A LIFETIME 12
3. FIRST GLIMPSE OF THE HIMALAYAS 20
4. THE 'TRUST WALK' 32
5. THE SECRET 49
6. AN UNBELIEVABLE ENCOUNTER 58
7. THE INTRUDER 71
8. NO WAY OUT 80
9. THE SEARCH BEGINS 90
10. GROPING IN THE DARK 102
11. BELOW FREEZING POINT 123
12. A HIDDEN WORLD OF SNOW 132
13. HOPING AGAINST HOPE 147
14. JOURNEY TO THE GOLDEN STAR ... 167
15. THE IMPENDING DANGER 181
16. LETHAL CLOUDS STRIKE 192
17. REACHING FOR THE STAR 208

DISCLAIMER

This is a work of fiction.
All characters, places, religious, social institutions and events in this novel are a creation of imagination.
Any resemblence to them in reality is purely coincidental

A JOURNEY BEGINS

A distant sound of chants echoed in his ears. Still weary, Steve strained to open his eyes. When had he fallen asleep? He could not remember. Where was he now? He looked around and found himself cramped in a corner of what looked like the dark interiors of a truck. There were about fifty other boys huddled together in that cold little space. He could hardly see their faces, in the darkness; but from what he could see, they appeared to be from around the world. Most of them were sleeping. Many must have traveled longer than what he had, he thought.

The mystical chants continued at a distance, punctuated by the reverberating sound of a gong. Steve could not decipher the language or the religious association, of the chants. All he could guess, from the sound, was that there was a large group of men, chanting in some closed space. The chants made no sense to him; but it filled him with beautiful calm, even in that miserable state.

But the calm was soon overtaken by the cramps in his stomach. There was still no sign of food. In the last twenty four hours, all he had got for food was a bowl of porridge and a dry bun. But, he was used to surviving on little food, after all those years in the Holy Family orphanage.

The orphanage building, in the dingy corner of a narrow lane, in the outskirts of New York, could have easily passed for a haunted house, in any film. Steve had learned to face the hardships in the confines of the damp walls of the orphanage. The room that he shared with eight other boys had just about enough space for each of them to spread a mattress and a hard pillow on the floor. Only when it rained, the space would seem a little less; because the leaking ceiling would not leave enough dry floors for all of them to sleep together.

For an eight year old, life had been a big challenge for Steve. In moments of loneliness he would imagine how life could be with parents around? He didn't know how it felt to cuddle up to his mother or piggy ride his father. This void always showed on him. His cute round face had a pair of glistening blue eyes. But those beautiful eyes were filled with sadness. His long golden hair that fell on his forehead was often carelessly combed. He was tall for his age, but lack of healthy food had made him lanky.

Inside the truck, as Steve curled further, digging his head into his knees, he thought of the orphanage room again. This was the exact position he would use to sleep in the winters, when the damp walls would feel like the interior of a cold storage. Although the half-inch mattress was hardly a shield, this curled-up position and four layers of 'donated' clothes made it a bit easier to brave the chilled floor.

Enduring that cold was probably easier than braving the pangs of hunger, which were becoming unbearable now. That's when Steve remembered something and dug into his bag. The tips of his fingers, peeping out of the torn gloves, were too numb to work through the bag. After some effort, he finally felt that familiar rough surface. Something he had almost forgotten about—that sweet bun!

An extra bun was a rare and eagerly awaited addition to Steve's otherwise meager diet at the orphanage. And this piece of dry bun was especially precious. After all, this bun was baked on a day that was to change the course of his life.

That day had not seemed too special, at first. It was just another day of working in the bakery—endlessly baking buns, just so that he could get his share of dinner that evening. His good friend David, an eight-year-old like Steve, worked with him at the oven, while the other boys worked at kneading the dough, shaping the buns, decorating, and packing them. It was Christmas time and the work had doubled; but David and Steve were thankful that the heat of the furnace helped to beat the biting December cold.

Although they used to bake hundreds every day, Steve and the other boys in the bakery almost never got to taste those fluffy dry fruit buns.

David could not stop himself this time, and whispered to Steve, "Hey Steve! This Christmas, the buns would taste extra yummy, wouldn't they?"

"How would I know?" said Steve, "We are here to 'bake' buns, not 'taste' them." "And why not?" This was John, who was new to the bakery. David smirked in reply, "Okay, go ahead."

John picked up one and was about to put it almost entirely into his mouth when Steve jumped in and snatched it away, "Have you lost it?" he said.

"What's the fuss about?" retorted an almost angry John.

Keeping the bun aside, Steve whispered to John "You've surely not met Mr. Arnold!"

Mr. Arnold was the Chief Warden of the Holy Family orphanage. His wife had died while delivering a stillborn child. Since then, all children filled him with the dreary despair of death. Unfortunately, for him as well as the children, he was stuck with the job at the orphanage. And this had only worsened his bitterness toward children. He could see only one way out of his hatred for children—to 'whip' it all out, quite literally.

Steve was continuing to warn John of Mr. Arnold's lashing, when he heard David scream, "Steve, the oven!"

Steve turned with fear; he had forgotten all about the buns that he had put into the oven, quite some time back. He froze as he saw the thick smoke wriggling out of the closed oven. He leaped toward the oven and scampered to open the lid. All the children looked on in horror, as the blackness of the smoke filled the room. Steve hurriedly took out the tray from the oven and squirmed as he saw it—a tray full of two dozen charcoaled buns! Not a word was spoken for a few minutes.

The smoke soon became unbearable. Choking and coughing, the children ran to the door. But, before they could breathe in some smoke-free air, their breaths were taken away by the sight in front of them!

It was the lean and looming figure of Mr. Arnold standing at the entrance to the bakery! The unshaven face of this forty-seven-year-old was partially covered with locks of salt-and-pepper hair, deliberately combed across to hide an errant bald patch, above the forehead. But, his baldness continued to defy him, at the back of his head, as it peaked through the tightly combed, greased-up hair, tied into an inch-long pony. The long, bushy hair on his ear, seen even from behind, seemed to compensate for the thinning hair on his head.

The right eye was partially covered with his hair; but the other eye could look through anyone from within its dark circles and bushy eyebrows. The heavy pouch, prominent under this eye, was acquired through years of compulsive drinking. The final accessory on this formidable face was a cheap cigar dangling from the corner of his lips.

That face, protruding out of a droopy set of shoulders, was the theme of many a nightmare at the orphanage. And that day looked like yet another of those days that were nightmares to be lived through. It was on that day that John, who was standing ahead of the others, got his first glimpse of that face; and he prayed that he would never see it again.

Steve, David, and the other kids stood still,

uncertain about Mr. Arnold's next move. There was an uneasy silence, as the black smoke gradually settled down, clearing the vision for Mr. Arnold to look at every boy standing there. As the smoke outside cleared, urgent, heavy puffs shot out of his lips, from either side of the cigar. Having scanned the rest of the boys, his eyes stopped at the new face standing right across him.

Mr. Arnold walked slowly toward John. Stooping over the boy, he blew a strong puff of smoke at that trembling face. John looked up through the smoke to see those piercing eyes and fuming nostrils. John felt like he would choke on that pungent smoke. Involuntarily, he coughed, covering his burning eyes with his palm. Tears rolled down as John rubbed his eyes.

Mr. Arnold grabbed him by his shoulders and shook him vigorously. Through all the shaking, John heard a hoarse voice screaming, "Oh stop, you! Stop coughing and putting on this weepy act of yours. So, we have yet another sissy in our midst. And what's the name of this one? You...you, I'm asking you?" Then, shouting louder "What-is-your-name?"

By this time, John had lost his voice. He tried hard, but could not speak. Well, Mr. Arnold did have a way of leaving an indelible first impression—an impression that penetrated deep into a boy's vulnerable soul and stayed there for the rest of his life. John was no exception. He stood there dumbfound, shivering under the suffocating clutches of Mr. Arnold, who had still not done with him.

"That's it you dumb nitwit!" And out came the

cane, with a swish of its leather tip. An encounter with Mr. Arnold was incomplete without a meeting with this faithful accomplice, which was tucked beneath his belt. Always by his side, like a sword.

Before John could register the full meaning of the sound of the cane, the roar from the smoke-filled mouth continued, "Out with your name! And the name of the ruffian who created this mess in my bakery!"

John was too terrified to do or say anything; while Mr. Arnold continued to lose his patience. "Listen, you...you wooden dodo! If you do not open your shut trap in the next few seconds, the rest of the talking will be done by my whip."

Saying this, he poked the leather tip of the cane into John's face. John had completely frozen by now. The only movement in his body was that of the tears that rolled down his cheek.

"Fine! You stubborn little fellow. Your countdown begins NOW! Ten - Nine - Eight - Seven...I just want your name. It couldn't be that hard!

"Six - Five - Four....Speak up! Three - Two...And, this is your last chance!"

There was pin drop silence as Mr. Arnold tightened his grip on his cane. The boys looked at one another in distress, praying that John would open his mouth. But he stood motionless, as the final number was rumbled out—"One!"

"That's it!" fumed Mr. Arnold. He raised his stick, as John shut his eyes tightly. He was about to strike, when a loud voice uttered, "John!" Mr. Arnold stopped and looked around to see who had dared to open his mouth.

"His name is John," said Steve, loud and clear. "Ah-ha! Of course, it's you, Steve—the leader of the gang," said Mr. Arnold, lowering his cane.

"So, here's the self appointed spokesperson for Mr. John. Will you please step forward, Mr. Defense Lawyer?"

Steve calmly went up and stood beside John. There was an uneasy silence, as Mr. Arnold wiped his cane on his pants, and reverently tucked it back under his belt.

Steve knew what to expect next. Mr. Arnold grabbed him by his collar and pulled him forward. Leaning down, he brought his face uncomfortably close to Steve's. Clutching his cigar with the corner of his lips, he spoke in a threateningly loud, husky whisper. "So, what exactly is wrong with your friend? Has 'Mr. John' lost his tongue or have his tonsils fallen off his vocal chord?"

Steve hated the way this man spoke, but replied calmly, "Mr. Arnold…John is…" but before he could complete his sentence the fuming warden shouted.

"Did I hear 'Mister,' again? You continue to defy me, when I have made it mighty clear that I should be called 'Sir.' I am not any 'mister' that you hell boys can mess around with. Call me 'Sir'…..

S - I - R…'Sir,' do you understand?"

"Ok, 'Sir'," said Steve, as he thought to himself "As if you've been knighted by some king!"

"Sir, John is new to this place," Steve spoke cautiously. "He doesn't speak much; not even to us. I think he got a little nervous around you. So..."

"So?" snapped Mr. Arnold, "Am I some kind of a beast whose presence should make this poor kitten nervous?"

"Yes, of course! You are the biggest beast around." That's exactly what Steve wanted to say; but he decided it was better to be quiet then.

"Ok, now, let's come to the point. Which one of you is responsible for creating this mess around here?" said Mr. Arnold, looking around menacingly. "Come up quickly, admit your crime, and get ready for the punishment; or else each one of you..."

"Sir, it's me," interjected Steve.

"I guessed as much." Picking up a blackened bun from the floor, Mr. Arnold added, "Who else could be as creative as the gang leader, himself?"

He sniffed at the bun. "Umm, what an aroma!" saying this he brought the bun very close to Steve's nose and said "Have you ever tried one of these 'Special dry fruit Christmas buns?'"

"No, sir," was the short answer.

"So, here is your chance of a lifetime. Go ahead; eat it!" said Mr. Arnold mocking at Steve.

"Sir, you know I can't eat this bun," replied Steve point blank.

Mr. Arnold's dark lips curled up into a crooked smile—while one side continued to hold the cigarette. "And why not?" he said, as he kept the bun pressed to Steve's lips.

Steve felt sickened by the bitter smell of the burned bun shoved under his nostrils. Trying to free himself from the choking odor and strangling grip, he managed to mumble, "Sir, they are burned."

"Oh, are they?" shouted Mr. Arnold. "Oh yes, they are burned. Not just burned, they've been ruthlessly charred. And if a ruffian like you can't eat it, how can you expect anyone else to buy it?

"Now, twenty four of these precious buns have been deliberately destroyed by this gang. You definitely don't deserve any dinner tonight. None of you!"

Having declared the sentence, Mr. Arnold turned to walk away, when Steve spoke again. "That's not fair, sir." That boy had the guts to speak up against his rule! Mr. Arnold turned around, furiously puffing at his cigar. "What did I hear you say? What was that, you little scoundrel?" said Mr. Arnold fuming. "It's not fair, sir," was Steve's frank reply. "Isn't it? So, what does You Honor think is fair?" Mr. Arnold shot back.

Steve stood silently, looking at the vindictive man who hated him the most. A couple of months back, Steve had complained against Mr. Arnold to a Trustee of the orphanage. The Trustees had other more profitable activities to manage, and did not want to get too involved in the day-to-day workings of the orphanage. But, they did pull up Mr. Arnold and reproached him sufficiently enough to rest their consciences for a while.

Today was Mr. Arnold's much awaited chance to avenge his pride. And he was not one to let an opportunity slip off his hands. He would surely teach that devil of a boy a golden lesson in obedience.

"Yes! Mr. Gang Leader," said Mr. Arnold, "what

is 'Fair'?"

"Sir, I am responsible for this. You can punish me, but not the others." Steve was soft, but firm.

"Fair enough!" shouted Mr. Arnold, with an evil glee peeping out of his eyes. "Fair enough, indeed!"

"Boys, your gracious gang leader has decided to take all your sins upon him. This filthy head is going to bear the crown of thorns. Well, then…the punishment should fit this noble filth. Let's see…the punishment for destroying and wasting twenty four valuable buns…what should it be?" As Mr. Arnold performed to his rooted audience, he looked around to note the frightened attention of every boy. "Burning twenty four buns...that definitely deserves twenty four perfect strokes of my cane. And, I'll also give you a choice! Take all twenty four on one hand, or make it easier, and take twelve on each palm. Twenty four strokes for twenty four buns. That's fair for sure!"

Some boys involuntarily let out muffled gasps. Until that day, "five strokes" was as much as any boy in that room had heard, or managed to bear. With renewed pride, Mr. Arnold took out his cane again, and went on with a self-pleased chant of "twenty four for twenty four." Steve remained silent. He quietly put forth both his palms. They were smeared with ash from the oven. Mr. Arnold looked at them with disgust. "Your palms are as filthy as you. Wash them well, after I'm done. Mr. Arnold turned to the boys, "Well, let's get started. Boys, you do the counting…1 to 24. Here goes!"

*

SHOCK OF A LIFETIME

The first stroke cracked on Steve's left palm—all of three inches long. He sat down wreathing in pain.

"Come on, get up." shouted Mr. Arnold. "Or, this will take ages. Now, let's see your right palm."

Steve stood up slowly, as he winced and stretched out his right hand. Mr. Arnold raised his stick but stopped mid-air. It was weird. He clearly remembered whipping the left palm. But, in front of him, he could see the right palm, glowing, and red hot.

"What kind of trick is this?" asked a bewildered Arnold. "Didn't I just hit your left palm? Are you trying to be smart, again? Show me your left palm...Now!"

Steve stretched out his left hand, beside the right. Mr. Arnold could see the distinct purple abrasion left by the cane. Back to the right palm...it was still glowing red! A confounded Mr. Arnold was losing his cool. "Forget this. Let's not waste any more time on this stupidity. Get ready boys. Here comes the second one! Say 'Twooooo!'"

And, once again the cane was raised. With a fierce swish, it darted to land on Steve's red palm. And then, it happened!

Steve was still not certain what exactly followed. He remembered flashes of some actions, and some sights. He remembered the cane coming down with a hiss and reaching his palm. But, he did not remember it hitting him.

Those who watched, have a vague memory of the cane landing on Steve's palm. What they remember clearly, however, is seeing Mr. Arnold flying across the room, as if struck by a thunderbolt. He hit the ceiling and came down crashing, on a rack of buns. First the buns fell on him, then the racks; and finally, the tins of dry fruits knocked him down. And 'sir' blacked out!

When Mr. Arnold opened his eyes, he found himself surrounded by the boys. Everyone looked bewildered.

As he staggered to stand up, he saw Steve standing away from the group. There, where he'd left him, Steve stood staring at his stretched out palms. As soon as he saw the boy and those wretched palms, he leaped up like he'd seen a ghost.

"Murderer!" he screamed, pointing at Steve. "He tried to murder me. He wanted to kill me!" Shouting like a mad man, he pushed his way out of the group that was crowded around him. He continued to scream, "Murderer," as he ran out of the bakery.

Awe-struck eyes followed the screaming, until he was out of their sight. Then, as if in an orchestrated move, all heads turned to Steve. He was still rooted there, staring at his palms in disbelief.

There was regrouping around the next spectacle—the notorious right palm. It looked normal. Not the slightest of hints of the cane's stroke was left on it. But, the left palm was swollen, with a deep scar in the middle. How one hand could be so badly affected, while the other remained stubbornly fine!

That night Steve burned in fever. The freezing floor made it worse. Shaken by the events of the day and the ceaseless pain in his left palm, he tossed without sleep. He wasn't given any dinner. The hunger made the shivering uncontrollable. He was trying to snuggle his head into his knees, when he heard voices that seemed to come from the hall. It sounded like some argument, and the volume was steadily increasing.

Steve quietly walked out of the room, across the corridor, toward the hall. The door of the hall was left slightly open—just enough for Steve to get a good peek into the room. He could clearly see the orphanage trustees gathered around a table. They were listening to someone, who seemed to be standing somewhere close to the door. Steve struggled to get a view of the speaker. It was Mr. Arnold—flaunting a bandage across his forehead, and gesticulating wildly.

"Yes!" he went on "Trust me; they've been conspiring for some time now. All the boys have been instigated. Their ears have been poisoned against me."

"To think that all this time, I gave up everything to care for them...and they were plotting to kill me! And, this was the blessed day that they unleashed their well-planned plot. It was only the grace of the good God that saved me. After all, He knows I've been working for these kids for so long." Mr. Arnold was determined to impress upon the trustees.

"And who do you think has been behind this plot? Surely, not one of the boys of this orphanage." said one of the trustees.

"Of course, one of them! He is very much part of this orphanage," said Mr. Arnold dramatically.

"That's preposterous, Arnold. These are six-to-eight-year-olds we're talking about," replied a member in disbelief.

"There's a lot that six- or eight-year-olds are capable of. It's all well for you to think every boy is innocent, just because he's young," continued Mr. Arnold who was determined to drive home his point. "I'm the one who lives with these boys. I see violence, hidden; just waiting for a chance. I see how they can..."

"Okay, that's enough! Who according to you is this plotting murderer?" asked a restless trustee.

There was a sense of fear rising in Steve, who was witnessing this drama from the door.

"The one who masquerades as a victim. A boy whom no one will ever suspect. A boy, who..."

"That's enough of suspense! Just spit out the name."

"It's STEVE!" announced Mr. Arnold.

Although Steve had suspected what was coming, he could not quite believe what he was hearing.

"Steve? Wait! Is this all because he complained against you?" asked one Trustee, while another clarified, "Steve, who?"

"Steve Brown," said another. "The boy, who said that this man ill-treats them, smokes at their faces, and what not! Come to think of it, Arnold, you do reek of smoke!"

"I don't deny that I enjoy an occasional smoke. Who does not? And, we've already been through this. We're talking about something more sinister here. A 'boy' tried to kill me. We're talking of someone who can do 'this' to me. Think of the influence he'd have on the other 'innocent' boys," Mr. Arnold completed his speech theatrically gesturing at his bandage.

"Somehow, I can't get myself to believe you," said another trustee.

"Don't you believe these scars, all over my body? These stitches on my forehead?" Mr. Arnold went on pointing all over his body. "Can this happen accidentally? A whole gang of boys, led by Steve attacked me in the most cold-blooded fashion. This matter should be handled seriously, and immediately."

"What do you suggest?" retorted an impatient listener.

"Well, we should do what is done in any other case of attempted murder. We should call the police," was Mr. Arnold's well-thought out answer.

Steve could feel his heart sink, and could not continue to look inside. As he lowered his head, he heard, "Have you lost your mind, Arnold? Police proceedings against a little kid?"

Another trustee continued, "And, what about our reputation? Police entering these premises…it'll be shameful. We can't allow that."

Mr. Arnold was not one to be subdued like this. "In that case, I will have to resign." Firmly, he continued, "I have served the orphanage all my life. And, I don't mind that you don't want to protect me. But, the kids...they're my responsibility. I cannot stay here, while I see a rotten apple spoiling them all. He's not meant for an orphanage. These sorts of boys need a good remand home. It'll be best for him!"

Steve felt like rushing in to tell the real story. He was about to push the door open, when a hand stopped him from behind. It was John. John shook his head strongly, pleading him not to go in; and, Steve relented.

Inside the hall, there was a long spate of silence, as the trustees stared at Mr. Arnold. Each looked at the other for some hint of how to proceed.

Finally the chairman, Mr. James Proctor, came up with a suggestion. "Last month I had received a letter from a Buddhist monastery situated somewhere in Northern India, in the Himalayan mountains. Apparently, they adopt orphans from all over the world, every year. They induct them into the monastery and bring them up as monks. I was not too sure about sending one of our boys so far away. We can't say how people will react if they come to know this. But, in this case, it might be best for all. And, we will, of course, keep this among ourselves."

The Chairman's suggestion was unanimously accepted. Mr. Arnold tried to hide a smile. Steve, behind the door, tried to hide a tear.

It was early next morning, when Steve was ready

with a small hand bag, stuffed with donated clothes. Most of the boys were sleeping, and would repent not having bid farewell to their dear friend. Only David and John were with him. As he walked out of the room, Steve turned to get a last glimpse of his roommates. He walked the length of the corridor with David and John, and was about to open the main door, when he heard a voice from behind.

"Steve! Come here, darling." This was Susan, the cook. The boys called this roly-poly looking, middle-aged lady, 'Aunt Susie,' who was the only source of real affection within the damp walls of the orphanage.

Susan took Steve to the kitchen and said, "I know you didn't do anything wrong. It's a dirty world in here. Maybe it's better for you to be going far away from here…to the other side of the world. I will always wish and pray for you." She hugged him and took out a dry fruit Christmas bun from the pocket of her apron.

"You have slogged all these days to bake hundreds of these, but never got to taste one. Here, keep this in your bag and eat it when you are hungry. Good bye my child." Susan turned away to hide her tears.

"Thank you, Aunt Susie," said Steve to himself, as he looked at the somewhat dry bun, which he had preserved in his bag. After that long and weary journey, nothing could be more welcome than his hand made 'Christmas bun.' He took a big bite at it. Each munch filled him with bitter-sweet memories of the orphanage, his friends, and the events that he had left behind. He continued to relive the chain of events that had brought him here, when a loud knock at the steel door of the truck startled him. He could hear voices outside the truck. "Come on, wake up. Wake up, boys." The other boys in the truck started stirring, slowly rising from their slumber.

The door of the truck was pushed open. There was an explosion of golden light in the darkness of the truck, as it was flooded by the bright morning sun. Along with the rays came in a light mist and a gentle, but chilly breeze. It was colder than Steve had ever experienced. The boys folded themselves tightly inside their jackets and jumped off the truck, one after another. Before he jumped, Steve peeped out of the truck. And, he stood right there…captivated by what he saw!

*

FIRST GLIMPSE OF THE HIMALAYAS

Steve's eyes drank in the sight—the majestic range of the Himalayas, spread all around him! In the glow of the early morning rays, the snowcapped mountains shined like molten gold.

Just above the foothills, almost one with the mountains was the quaint structure of a Buddhist monastery. Bright red and maroon tapering roofs rested on huge pillars and snow white walls. And surrounding this beautiful structure, were pine trees that spread for miles. These trees seemed to extend all the way into to the clouds. And the leaves, they looked so fresh; as if they had just been sparkle-cleaned.

Now the chanting was clearer. What Steve had heard inside the truck was coming from the monastery in front of him. Steve imagined that there must be a large group of people, inside a huge hall. His body was now resonating with the mesmerizing harmony. It was as if his pulse was moving with the rhythm of the chanting.

Mantra after mantra, emanating from the monastery, seemed to dissolve among the pine trees, rise up to the mountains and return to him, soothing all the pain that he had ever experienced. "Was this the house of God?" thought Steve as he felt gripped by some kind of love.

Then, from the memories of his not-so-love-filled days, popped out a familiar image—that of the Holy Family orphanage and the concrete jungle of New York. He looked forward to a different, if not better, life here.

Steve stood there, seized by the beauty of the sounds and sights, when someone touched his shoulder, gently. At first he did not notice, because he was not used to a soft touch. When he was tapped again, he turned and saw a young monk smiling at him. Draped in a long maroon dress that looked like a gown, this gentle person looked serene in his shaven head. He spoke softly, "What are you thinking?"

Steve was in deep thoughts and yet was blank. Lost in these surroundings, he did not know what to say. "Yeah, kind of thinking. But…don't know what!"

"Think good thoughts, and good things will happen to you. Come, let's go," said the monk, and he guided Steve toward the monastery.

The narrow pebbled path leading down to the monastery was lined with tall pine trees. The wind and mist that rustled through the leaves carried the fragrance of some wild flowers. The bushes on the side of the pebbled path were bathed in dew drops, which glistened like pearls in the morning sun. Butterflies that fluttered around, occasionally brushed against Steve. A few steps away, he noticed a tiny bird struggling to fly. Its weak wings were not yet ready to soar. The monk saw the bird, picked it up, and softly placed it in its nest.

By now they had reached the large courtyard in front of the monastery. The magnificent building looked even more impressive now. The tiled roof was lined with saffron flags that fluttered in the soft breeze, in a harmonious rhythm.

Along the wall were large cylindrical, metal structures. These brightly painted cylinders had some scriptures inscribed in gold. A group of young monks walked past the cylinders, rolling them with a gentle touch. As the cylinders rolled, they produced a humming sound that echoed all over the valley. The young monks made two rows on both sides of a huge door, which was closed. They lit a bunch of large incense sticks and started waving them in the air. The whole atmosphere was filled with a mystical fragrance, as the young monks started chanting. The humming of the cylinders, the chanting of the young monks, and the fragrance of the incense sticks created an ambience of absolute peace. Steve felt one with the universe, spellbound by all that was happening around him, when a loud droning sound drew him out of his trance. He looked around and saw two groups of monks carrying two large trumpet-like instruments. The instruments were about six-or-seven-feet long—broad at one end and tapered at the other, resembling the trunk of an elephant. Each trumpet was being carried by four monks, on their shoulders. One person, who walked behind them, was blowing into the trumpet. The sound was long and hollow, and its vibrations seemed to tug somewhere deep at Steve's heart. All the groups of monks—the incense burners, the trumpet carriers, the chanters—formed rows along the pathway that led to the main door of the monastery building. The droning trumpets and the synchronized chanting grew louder as if summoning the doors to open. They were all waiting for someone.

Steve's eyes were fixed at the huge doors as he wondered who was about to emerge from within. The other boys who had traveled with him were getting impatient. Suddenly a big gong was sounded and the majestic doors of the monastery opened slowly. Steve got a glimpse of the interior of the monastery. He could see a wide and high-ceilinged hall, lit up with hundreds of lamps. The brightly painted walls glowed with the lamps.

As the doors opened wider, the lamps started to flicker with the wind. In the dancing lights, the dragons and other figures painted on the walls seemed to move. As Steve enjoyed the play of the lamps inside the hall, he noticed a long corridor that stretched beyond the hall. At the end of the corridor, he could make out the figures of four men moving toward the door. They were holding the ends of a large white cloth that was spread out like a movie screen. As the men moved closer, the cloth sparkled with flickering violet spots, as if the back of the cloth was lined with tiny lights, like those adorning a

Christmas tree. As they reached the door, Steve could see that the men holding the glittering white curtain were monks.

At the door, the curtain was lowered, but there were no flickering violet lights. What appeared from behind was an old Buddhist monk who seemed to have the kindest eyes and the most loving smile that Steve had ever seen. As soon as the old monk appeared, the sound of the trumpets and the chanting stopped. The silence in the courtyard was immediately taken over by the chirping of birds, as the old monk walked toward the boys. Steve thought that there was something weird about the walk. As he gazed down, he realized that the monks' feet were not touching the ground. He seemed to be floating, a few inches above the earth. Like Steve, the other boys stared at the monk's feet in disbelief. For the first time since they got off the truck, the boys felt a little scared.

But as soon as the old monk spoke, every fear of every boy melted into a pure and quiet joy. "My beloved children, welcome to the abode of Love—the Gompa! In this house of God, there is no anger, there is no fear. Everyone is loved, everyone is dear! From today you enter a world devoid of hatred, jealousy, judgment, or violence. Here, we are all children of God; we live and spread the message of Love. Welcome to God's land!"

The kind voice bathed the boys in love. Some of them, including Steve, could not hold back their tears. A monk standing nearby gently wiped Steve's face. A drop of tear glistened on the monk's finger like a gem in the rays of the morning sun. Showing Steve the sparkling tear, the monk said, "These are precious diamonds. From this moment, they will never flow out of pain. Preserve them and spread the message of Happiness and Love!"

The monk then gestured with his eyes to revert his attention to the old leader, who went on to give a brief message about Love. This was followed by a ceremony for initiating the boys into the monastery. Two monks lit some incense sticks inside a perforated silver bowl. They then asked the boys to come and stand before the old monk, one at a time.

Every time a boy came forward, the monk would first move the incense bowl around the boy's body, to encircle him in white smoke. Later, Steve would learn that this "smoke bathing" ritual was to purify the aura of the new boys. But right then, Steve could only see that the smoke from the incense bowl was somehow making the boys feel lighter and freer. After the smoke ritual, a spoonful of fresh, spring water was poured into the palm of the initiate. After sipping the water, the boy was taken into the monastery.

Steve was the last boy in the row. He had been watching the rituals patiently and felt a sense of calm, deep within. He walked up to the old monk and looked at his serene face. This aging face had something uncommon about it. Although the lines on the face seemed regular, those on his forehead looked peculiar. As the monk bent to bless him, Steve got a closer look. He saw that the lines on the monk's forehead looked like the stem of a blooming lotus, whose thousand petals were spread across his shaven head.

The old monk's kind eyes were smiling at Steve, as he asked for the bowl of incense smoke. Steve looked at the exquisite silver bowl, which had some religious engravings on it. It was covered by a perforated silver lid. The smoke was coming out of the small holes in the lid. It was tied to a delicate silver chain which was held by the old monk.

"Close your eyes," said the monk to Steve as he started to turn it around Steve's head in circles. Steve reverently shut his eyes, as the smoke encircled his body.

There was a sigh of astonishment in the group that was watching, as the white smoke started turning violet around Steve's forehead. As the incense bowl was lowered along Steve's body, the smoke turned from violet to indigo to blue, green, yellow, orange, and red. Everyone watched this wonderful sight in complete silence. The old monk closed his eyes and meditated in silence. After a few moments, he looked at Steve and spoke softly, "Open your eyes, Steve!"

Steve felt as if he had woken up from a deep slumber. He suddenly realized that the monk had called him by his name. How could the monk know his name?

He looked up, bewildered, into the old monk's eyes. Those kind eyes had turned blue, as though they were holding the deep waters of the oceans inside them.

"Steve, my child! I am Shom. For ages I have waited for you to come to me. Finally that day is here." He looked up into the sky and said, "Thank you, my Lord!"

Steve could not believe his ears. How could someone speak without opening his mouth? And he felt as if he had heard the voice not in his ear, but in his heart. He kept looking at the monk, in complete admiration, as Shom took a spoonful of spring water and said, "Show me your right palm, Steve."

Steve was immediately reminded of the incident when his right palm had strangely caused Mr. Arnold to be darted across the room, like a tennis ball. That one unexplainable incident had changed the course of his life. He did not want anything of that sort to happen again. So, he stood there without moving his hands.

"What happened, Steve?" asked Shom "What are you thinking? Have no fear. You will only be given some water to drink."

After a moment's hesitation Steve extended his left hand. At this, Shom was amused. He said, "My child, this is Holy Water. You should drink it from your right palm."

Steve started rubbing his perspiring right palm on his trouser, to clean it as much as he could. He had not forgotten the number of times he had been abused for keeping his palms dirty. Having rubbed it clean, Steve, reluctantly, produced his right palm. Shom uttered some holy words into the spring water and was about to put it into Steve's right palm, when he stopped. Steve followed Shom's shocked gaze.

Shom was staring at Steve's palm, which had started glowing. In the middle of the palm, emerged seven curved lines, bearing the seven colors of the rainbow. As Shom looked on, at the play of rainbow colors, tears of joy rolled down his eyes. He bent down and kissed Steve's palm.

"You are the chosen one, my child! You will bring about the change this world is waiting for." Shom's voice was shaking with tender excitement, as he hugged Steve. Steve drank the Holy Water. It was water, but so sweet.

"You are holier than any holy water. Come with me." Shom held Steve's hand and took him to a pathway that meandered from the right of the monastery, somewhere into the pine trees. The two continued to walk toward the woods, leaving behind a baffled group of young monks, who wondered what Shom was doing. None of them knew what Shom had seen; neither had they been able to hear what he had said.

Shom led Steve through the pathway, to a long staircase that ended in a garden lush with colors. As far as Steve's eyes could see, there were thousands of flower beds. A narrow path through the flower beds led to a small arch made of creepers. The arch seemed to lead into an enclosure of some kind. On top of the arch was a board made of flowers. It read, "Butterfly Nest."

Steve had never heard of butterflies building nests. He wondered how a butterfly nest would look like, if it did exist. He entered with Shom, through the arch, into a dimly lit passage. He could feel the softness of some breeze blowing from all directions, as if there were small fans fitted around the passage. Although it was rather dark, Steve could feel that the passage was abuzz with some kind of activity or motion.

As the passage ended, they entered a large space

that was enveloped by a huge dome. It was the most colorful, beautiful, and incredible sight that Steve had ever seen. He soon realized that the dome was made of neither cement nor concrete, neither glass nor creepers, nor any other material. The entire span of the humungous dome was made by millions and millions of butterflies. The soft breeze that was blowing from all directions was the fluttering of the wings of these butterflies. On the ground were beautiful plants made of tiny gems. Shom guided Steve to the center of the dome, to a bench made of leaves. As they sat on the bench, it sunk like soft cushion. Shom watched Steve totally lost in the wonder of the magical dome.

"Are you happy?" Shom broke the silence.

Steve was so awestruck that he did not hear Shom. He stared at the amazing dome that resembled a kaleidoscope, changing forms and shades, every time the butterflies moved. Unable to believe his eyes, Steve asked, "Are these real butterflies?"

Shom smiled, "Why do you ask that?"

Steve kept looking up, "I had never imagined that there were so many butterflies in the world. And if there were, how could they all gather at one place?"

Shom looked at the little boy, full of love. "There are many more butterflies, in every corner of the world. But there are very few people who know about them. These butterflies are born here. You see these glittering gems? They are butterfly eggs that will turn into beautiful butterflies in a few days, and the Butterfly Nest will grow bigger."

"But, butterflies always sit on flowers," said

Steve. "I don't see any flowers up there. What are they holding on to?

"You are right, Steve." said Shom, "There are no flowers anywhere in this dome. They are holding on to one another. Or should I say, just flying along, with one another."

"Why don't they fly away?" Steve was still perplexed.

"Like all of us, they are here on earth with a purpose." explained Shom, "They are performing their duty of guarding a great secret. Today, no one in the world knows this secret except me. I am at one end of this secret. And at the other end, Steve, are 'You'!"

Shom could sense that his words were confusing Steve. So, he added, "Don't worry, it's not that serious a matter. I brought you here so that you can make friends with these butterflies." Shom looked up, as if talking to the butterflies, "Friends, Would you not like to welcome Steve?"

Soon, a bunch of wondrous little butterflies surrounded Steve. Some of them perched on his shoulder and hair. A tiny one sat on his nose! Steve was amused. "You must be tired," he said, "Your friends will lead you to your room. Go, relax, mingle with your other friends, and enjoy yourself. Just remember, the 'Secret' is not to be shared. Only some of us in the monastery know about it."

Shom bid Steve goodbye and fondly watched him follow the butterflies out of the dome.

The butterflies led Steve through the fragrant garden, then the pine trees, to the large courtyard where the initiation rituals had been performed. Then, for the first time, Steve entered Gompa—the monastery. As he walked into the outer hall, he noticed that there were no electric bulbs in there. Beautiful oil lamps illuminated the entire space with a gentle yellow light. The walls and the roof were painted in bright colors with figures of humans and animals, birds and dragons. The roof was supported by four strong pillars. Buddhist Scriptures were etched in gold on these pillars. In front of Steve, a large part of the wall was covered by two huge curtains made of white cloth. It looked like the cloth was covering or hiding something. Steve wondered what.

He looked around. There was no one in the hall. He slowly walked toward the wall. In front of the white curtain was a small marble stand carrying a marble lotus, whose petals were closed. When he reached the lotus, Steve thought he heard a gurgling sound, as if a fountain was flowing inside the lotus. Standing alone in the middle of the huge mystical hall, with larger than life paintings that seemed to come alive; a mysterious gurgling sound coming from inside a lotus made of marble; huge white curtains hiding something; and not a soul around—Steve was a bit scared and confused. He did not know where to go, what to do next?

"What are you thinking?" A voice, though soft as a baby's, jolted him up. He quickly retreated from the marble lotus and looked around to see where the voice came from. There was no one there.

*

THE 'TRUST WALK'

"Don't be scared Steve. We all love you here." The childlike voice was so soft and so close to him that Steve wondered why he could not see anyone.

Steve mustered some courage, "Who are you? And why are you hiding?"

"I am not hiding. Look carefully, I am very close to you." The voice almost whispered into his ear.

"If you are so close, why don't you show up? Are you invisible?" asked Steve, trying to scan every inch of that hall.

"No, I am very visible and very close to you. But, you are looking very far. I am not on the walls or the ceiling."

Steve was beginning to get irritated. He looked very carefully at the pillars, the curtains, and even the white marble lotus in front of him. There was no sign of anyone.

"This is not fair," he said "you are playing tricks with me. I give up."

"Why do you give up so easily? I am so close." said the voice, almost into his ear.

"But, Where On Earth Are You?!" said Steve, finally raising his voice.

"On your shoulder," was the short-and-sweet reply.

Steve looked to his left. There was no one. When he turned to his right, he was stunned to see a pink butterfly, which was actually smiling at him. Steve was taken aback. Seeing him react, the butterfly flew from his shoulder and started fluttering in front of him. "Hi! I am Pinkoo! Master likes the pink color that I've been adorned with; so he calls me by this name. And you are Steve. Right?" said the butterfly.

"Yes! I am...But, you! How...how can you speak?" said Steve in bewilderment.

"Well, all butterflies speak. But not everyone can hear us...only the monks in this monastery and God's chosen people." Then, Pinkoo added, "Now we have to go into the Gompa. But, before that, pay your respects to Lord Buddha."

"Lord Buddha? Where is he?" asked Steve.

"See that white lotus in front of you," said Pinkoo, "touch it with your forehead."

Steve touched his forehead on the marble lotus. As he lifted his face, he felt the petals moving. To his surprise, the marble lotus started opening and soon it bloomed into a beautiful white lotus. At the center of the bloomed lotus, instead of pollen, was crystal clear blue water. Steve gazed at his reflection in the water, which was flowing like a spring; that's what created the soft gurgling sound.

Pinkoo flew and sat on a petal. "Now, put this water on your eyes." Steve dipped his finger in the water and applied it to his eyes. The water seeped into his eyes leaving a soothing and calming effect. When he opened his eyes he was amazed to see that hundreds of lamps, all around the wall, had started burning, though nobody lit them. As he looked up, the white curtains moved to either side to reveal an imposing gold statue of Lord Buddha. Buddha looked like he was meditating; in a yogic posture. Steve bowed before this calm, inspiring statue.

Pinkoo signaled him with her wing and said "Come with me," and flew toward a corner of the hall. Steve followed her. Pinkoo flew up and perched herself on a painted door on the wall. "Come up" said Pinkoo.

"How can I come up this wall? I can't fly like you" he said.

"I know you are not a butterfly," said Pinkoo. "But, you can climb up. See those stairs?"

She was pointing to a painting of a spiral staircase on the wall. This staircase led to the painted door.

"Poor Pinkoo, she thinks I can climb this painting. But, there is no point arguing with this supernatural creature," thought Steve and touched his foot on the first step of the painting. The next moment, the spiral stair case came out of the painting. In complete wonder, Steve climbed and reached the door. Pinkoo was smiling at the door, "So, was that difficult?" Steve was too awestruck to reply.

Pinkoo led him into a dormitory where Steve saw the other boys who had traveled with him. It was a cozy room. Each boy had a comfortable bed and a small cupboard.

The boys were taken to a large hall, where everybody squatted on the floor to eat. Although the lunch was very different from what he had eaten before, it felt wholesome.

After lunch, Steve spent an hour getting acquainted with the boys. The boys were busy sharing their experiences, when an elderly monk walked in and asked, "Hello boys! How about going for a trek?" Everyone jumped at the idea.

The excited initiates started on their first trek through the wondrous Himalayas. They walked across fields and tiny brooks on their way. Everything about the trek was enchanting—the misty green of the Himalayan valley, the gurgling of the brooks, the slight chill in the wind, the sweet fragrance of flowers that accompanied the wind.

When they reached the foot of a hill, they were asked to halt for a while. There, a senior monk—the trek leader—started with the instructions on how to procced. "Now we begin the most interesting part of our trek. It is called the 'Trust Walk.' We need to trek to the top of this hill, where a surprise awaits all of you."

As the boys murmured to each other in excitement, the monk interjected. "Wait, that's not it. All of you will be blindfolded." He was speaking to the new boys.

The tone of the murmuring shifted from excitement to surprise, and a tinge of fear. The monk pointed to the young monks, saying "Don't worry; one of these monks will accompany each of you. But, when you are blindfolded, you need to surrender yourself completely to the monk who is with you. You need to put all your faith on him." Then, speaking to the little monks, he said "On your part, you need to make sure that your partner is safe." Then, motivating the entire group, he said, "So, are you ready for the Trust Walk?"

The boys were not certain; but the task sounded interesting.

First, the boys had to choose their partners. In each pair, it was the experienced monk's duty to blindfold his partner with a strip of black cloth.

A young Nepalese monk, who seemed to be of almost the same age as Steve, walked up to him and said, "Hi, I am Cheeka. Can I be your partner?"

"Sure. My name is Steve." Steve immediately grew fond of Cheeka's smile—one that started from his eyes, which would wrinkle into narrow slits with the force of the smile. He had a cute face on which a tiny pink nose rested in between chuby pink cheek. A pair of twinkling black eyes that always seemed gleaming with excitement. His short black hair always seemed to stand up with excitement making him look like a cute baby porcupine.

Cheeka seemed as excited as Steve to go on the trek...which was why Steve was surprised to hear what Cheeka said next. "You know Steve; I have been on this Trust Walk many times. And every time, it's a new experience." Cheeka moved his gaze from the top of the hill to Steve and said, "So, are you ready?"

Steve was a bit nervous. "Yeah, sort of..."

"Don't worry; have faith in me. I promise I will

not let you down."

Steve took a while before he responded. "Okay, I trust you. You can put the blindfold now." Steve was about to close his eyes when an unusual sight caught his attention. He saw a bunch of bats hover a little above his head, in a rhythmic cycle.

"What happened?' asked Cheeka, as he found Steve perturbed.

"Did you notice those bats?' asked Steve. "I find something unnatural about them."

Cheeka looked up. But by then the bats had disappeared. "I don't see any bats here," he said, a bit perplexed. Steve was very sure that he had seen the bats. He looked blank. Cheeka sensed his state of mind and cheered him up.

"Forget it, friend," he said. "Let's get on with our game." Putting the blindfold on Steve's eyes Cheeka said, "You know something, Steve. They have not yet told you about an interesting part of this trek. On our way back, I will be blindfolded and you will guide me."

"Wow! I guess that would complete my role as your partner. But, I must confess I'm not as confident as you about how good a guide I'd be."

"I'm confident! You'd be great." By now the blindfold was tied. Cheeka asked, "Are you okay? Hope it's not too tight."

"It's just fine," said Steve feeling the blindfold.

"Okay. Can you wait a minute, while I check about what else we need to take with us?" said Cheeka looking around.

"Sure, I'll be fine," replied Steve. "I'm all ready to

go!"

"Good luck, then!"

"Thanks," said Steve, but soon realized that it was not Cheeka's voice.

"Wish me good luck, too," continued the other voice. Steve thought he recognized the voice, but did not think that it could be her! He pulled down his blindfold and peeped from one eye to confirm his guess.

"You!" said Steve. "What are you doing here, Pinkoo?"

"Why?" asked Pinkoo, "Can't I go on a Trust Walk with you? Master asked me to accompany you wherever you go."

After introducing her to Cheeka, Steve said, "Pinkoo, if you are coming for the Trust Walk, where is your blindfold?"

"Here," saying this, Pinkoo plucked a hair off Steve's head.

"Ouch!" whispered Steve, "what are you up to?"

"Just watch!" In all seriousness, Pinkoo took Steve's hair and tied it around her eyes. "Now I am ready. I am putting all my trust in you, partner. Blindfolded, I sit on your shoulder. I will go, wherever you go."

"You are crazy," Steve said with a laugh.

"Are you boys ready?" the loud voice of the trek leader alerted everyone. "Good luck to you all! Enjoy the Trust Walk."

Steve quickly adjusted his blindfold, as Cheeka ran back to him. Steve held Cheeka's hand and started walking with his support. While he could not see because of the blindfold, he felt like his sense of sound and smell was getting sharper. He could hear the sound of various birds and insects. He could hear his own footsteps and those of Cheeka and his other companions. He could even hear and feel the occasional flapping of Pinkoo's wings, close to his ear. He could feel Cheeka's hand holding him firmly.

Cheeka kept talking to him, telling him whether he should go right or left; whether he should take a long or a short step, depending on what was lying on the path ahead.

Although Steve was listening carefully to what Cheeka was saying, he was relying more on his own judgment. All his senses were alert and making sure that he was safe. Until this day, his keen senses had helped him to fend for himself. That's how he had survived the orphanage. Even now he trusted himself more than Cheeka, for surviving the trek.

At a distance, he heard the gurgling sound of flowing water. "We are approaching a small brook," explained Cheeka. "From here on, our path is full of slippery pebbles. You need to walk cautiously."

As they came to the bank of the brook, Cheeka told Steve, "This brook is not too wide. The water in the middle is knee deep. If we walk slowly, we'll be able to cross easily."

It was a bit colder near the brook, and Steve did not want to wet his shoes and socks. From what Cheeka said, he thought that he could jump over the brook.

"I think I can jump over the brook," said Steve.

Cheeka did not like the idea. "No Steve, it's risky.

Remember, you are blindfolded."

Steve was getting impatient. He let go of Cheeka's hand, while a panicked Cheeka remarked, "No Steve don't...don't jump!"

Steve had already jumped and he fell into the middle of the brook. The water was shallow, so he did not drown. But, all his clothes were drenched.

As he staggered to his feet, Steve heard a voice chide him, kindly. "You have betrayed Cheeka's trust."

It was his Master, Shom's voice. "Why did you lose patience, my child? If you can not surrender yourself to your friend, who is holding your hand, how can you surrender to God, whom you do not see? And you forgot, my child, that someone else was totally surrendered to you."

"Pinkoo!" Steve suddenly remembered that Pinkoo had blindfolded herself for the trust walk and was sitting on his shoulder. "Oh my God, where is Pinkoo?"

"I am here, sitting on your head," said Pinkoo's voice. "Don't worry", I am fine. Thank God, I am not wet, otherwise..."

By then, Cheeka rushed to the middle of the brook and quickly held Steve's hand. "Are you okay, Steve?"

"Yes, I am okay, Cheeka. That was stupid of me. I am really sorry, my friend," said a dejected Steve.

"Never mind," assured Cheeka. "We are partners. Let's move on!"

"Yeah! Let's go! Let's go!!" Steve heard an excited voice coming from the top of his head.

The rest of the trek seemed much lighter for Steve who had now absolutely surrendered to Cheeka. What a sense of freedom it was to be guided by another person; not having to bother about the next step! Steve was only worried about his wet clothes, especially because he expected it to get colder, as they climbed higher. But, surprisingly, as they approached the top of the hill, the air became warmer.

As the group reached the top of the hill, the new boys waited with bated breaths for their blindfolds to be opened. Steve could hear the sound of gushing water at a distance.

Finally, the trek leader announced, "Here we are boys. I must say each of you did exceedingly well in the Trust Walk. Now, your partners will take off your blindfolds, so that you can see the marvelous sight that is in front of you."

Cheeka slowly untied the blindfold off Steve. As Steve's eyes adjusted to the light, they saw it—that waterfall. No, it was not just another stream bouncing down a mountain. For, the entire waterfall was wrapped in a misty haze. It was like a heavenly group of millions of pristine, water droplets, bouncing like tiny, silver-white angels, with glowing halos around their heads. Everything looked heavenly in the backdrop of a clouded sky.

It took some time for Steve to realize that the mist was caused by the hot vapor from the waterfall, which was spreading warmth around it.

"Isn't it beautiful, Steve?" said Cheeka.

Steve was so lost in the sight that he forgot to

reply. Then, he heard that familiar voice again. "I've taken off my blindfold too." Pinkoo placed the hair that she had plucked off back on to Steve's scalp. "Oh, my-my! Isn't this gorgeous?" retorted Pinkoo.

"So this is your first visit too?" asked Steve.

"No, the hundred and twentieth visit." said Pinkoo casually. "But you know, every time I come here, I feel like it's the first time." Then, she added sadly, "Like every one of those times that I've come here, I can't go beyond this point. I can't wet my wings. I will play around while you go and have dip."

Steve watched Pinkoo fly away; then he turned to Cheeka in gratitude. "How can I thank you, partner? You have given me the most memorable experience of my life." Steve hugged Cheeka. In the meantime the sun came out of the clouds and formed a beautiful rainbow across the waterfall.

As Steve looked at the rainbow, a strange feeling started overpowering him. It seemed to start from his right palm. He looked down at it to see that it was glowing. A hot flash ran through his right hand and spread all over his body. Steve felt his temperature rising. Cheeka, who was holding Steve's hand, could feel the change in his body temperature. Feeling concerned, Cheeka asked "Are you ok, Steve? You seem to have fever."

There was no answer; so Cheeka turned to look at Steve, whose eyes were fixed on the rainbow. Meanwhile, the clouds covered the sun again, and the rainbow disappeared. Steve was back to normal. "What's wrong with you Steve?" Cheeka asked again.

"Why? Nothing; I mean, I don't know," replied

Steve, a bit confused.

"Maybe you caught a chill, when you fell into the brook." said Cheeka.

"I don't think so. I am fine," said Steve, trying to forget the incident. "Come, let's go for a warm dip."

As they ran into the warm water, they forgot all about what had happened. In all those years, Steve had never had such a refreshing shower. The water was so warm that it took away all the fatigue from his body. "This waterfall comes from the snow capped mountains. It should be freezing. How come it's so hot?" Steve asked Cheeka.

"Actually it's a rare waterfall that originates from a natural spring," explained Cheeka. "The rich sulfur content and other minerals make the water hot and good for health."

After a rejuvenating bath and all the fun and frolic at the waterfall, the kids were ravishingly hungry. And the food was inviting too. There were Momos—a local delicacy made of steamed rice flour and stuffed with vegetables. Then, there were boiled potatoes and vegetables sprinkled with mild Indian spices...all the food steaming hot from the hot case. And to wash it down, there was a tall glass of salty butter tea. The food was plentiful and the children could take as many helpings as they wanted.

All of them attacked the food hungrily. But Steve sat quietly, looking at the spread. He had not seen so much food in his life. In fact, he did not know the taste of most of the dishes. Although the kids at the orphanage baked exotic cakes and pastries, they were reserved for the Trustees or Mr. Arnold. To taste a slice of cake would mean stealing it. But that was too much of a risk, because the punishment was unbearable, if one were caught. So Steve sat there wondering which dish to 'touch!' That's when he heard Pinkoo's voice again, "What are you thinking?"

"Oh! You startled me, again!" said Steve. "How do you always manage to appear at the wrong time?"

"Or, is it the right time?" Pinkoo knew that Steve needed her help.

"Yeah, maybe...you're somewhat right," said Steve, reluctantly; he was not used to being open about his feelings.

Pinkoo started with her advice. "When you are hungry, don't think. The food is for all of us. See, I've got my share." Pinkoo had managed to get a chocolate chip from the cake and was enjoying it. She fluttered her wings against his hands and said "What are you waiting for? Go for it!"

Steve left his dark past behind. The next moment he was gorging at the delicious food. Cheeka gave Steve an almond chocolate that he had made himself, at the monastery. Steve was assured that he was in the company of loving people and good times were ahead of him. His first day in the monastery had washed away all his pain.

It was night. A beautiful moon peeped out of the window and Steve's bed seemed to be bathed in moonlight. Steve was looking at the beautiful moon, when he noticed the same bunch of bats, he had seen at the trek, hovering near his window. To see those black bats in the dead of the night was a frightful sight. Steve was too scared even to close the window.

Just then an owl hooted and the bats suddenly disappeared. Steve was relieved.

Lying on his soft bed he looked at the calm moon and thanked God for all the happiness he had been granted. He thought of his companions and friends back home, at the orphanage. How he wished that they could come out of the hell hole and live a blissful life here. Thinking about their pain made him sad. He was also reminded of Christmas which was not too far. Even though there was no great celebration for the boys at the orphanage, yet it was a day which was awaited through the year. May be this year Christmas would come and go without a celebration for him. Steve was deep in these thoughts, when he felt a soft touch on his shoulder. He turned and saw his Master smiling at him. His touch was always so soothing.

"So, how was your day, Steve?" asked Shom.

"I have never been so happy, all my life," Steve replied. "So much has happened in just one day. The Butterfly Nest, the Trust Walk...and then, the waterfall—more beautiful than anything I have ever imagined. But, something happened there. I don't understand what it was. It made me very uneasy, Master!" Steve stopped. He was trying to recollect exactly how he felt, when he saw the rainbow.

"What happened to you was perfectly normal," said Shom. "Go on."

"I was standing on top of the hill, with Cheeka and Pinkoo, watching the waterfall. I was happy. Everything was fine, until I saw a rainbow in the middle of the waterfall. I felt like I was being sucked into those colors. Everything around me—the waterfall, the trees, my friends—everything in sight was getting lost into some darkness. The only thing that remained was the rainbow in front of me. Nothing else seemed to exist. The rainbow seemed to grow bigger and brighter. Then, my body started reacting to the colors of the rainbow. First my right palm felt hot, as if it was glowing from inside. The heat started travelling up my right arm and spread very fast, all over my body. I felt like I had a high fever. But I did not feel week, like in a fever. I felt stronger and stronger; so powerful that I did not know what to do next. I was scared. But thank God, the sun went behind the clouds. The rainbow disappeared and within the next second, everything was back to normal…as if nothing had happened!" As Steve narrated the incident, huge drops of perspiration appeared on his forehead. He was breathing heavily.

Shom was sitting quietly beside Steve. He wiped the perspiration off Steve's forehead and hugged him. There was such magic in his Master's hug that Steve calmed down immediately.

"Steve, you are the most wonderful child of God. And trust me, whatever happened to you was absolutely normal. For anyone else, it would have been alarming. But you are different from others. You are special, my child!" Shom said with his ever-loving smile. "Now, can I see your right hand?"

Steve showed his hand. Shom looked at it carefully and said, "Look at the lines of your right palm. These seven curved lines, at the center of your palm, form a rainbow. And this is not a coincidence.

Now watch this carefully." Shom closed his eyes and silently uttered some mantras. After a few moments, he took a deep breath and blew gently on Steve's palm. And then, it happened! The seven lines on his palm started glowing with the seven colors of the rainbow. At first, Steve kept looking at the rainbow in disbelief. Gradually the glow of the rainbow became brighter, and even brighter. Steve felt that he was getting sucked into the glowing rainbow on his palm. His body temperature started rising, once again, giving him that feeling of immense power. The glow was so strong that it illumined the whole room. Steve's face was flushed, as though there was a spirit made of light growing inside him. Shom kept watching Steve and continued chanting. Finally, he closed Steve's palm and softly blew on his clenched fist. Slowly the glow disappeared and Steve was back to normal. Steve loosened his fist and started breathing normally. Shom took Steve in his arms and caressed his hair.

"What was all this, Master?" Steve asked in his confusion. "Are you a magician?"

Shom smiled. "No, my son. This is not magic. It's real."

"But I can't make anything out of this." Steve was not able to forget that feeling, that mystical experience. "Please help me, master!"

With an affectionate smile, Shom said, "Sometimes we do not understand the purpose for which God has sent us to this earth. Right now, I can only say that this rainbow, with which you are born, is for the good of humanity. It will never harm you.

You will realize its power very soon."

"Of course, you need to learn more about yourself and this world. Tomorrow, we will meet before sunrise, at the Butterfly Nest. Someone will escort you there. It's getting late now. Sleep well, my child. Good Night." Saying this, Shom touched Steve's forehead with his thumb. It made Steve very calm and sleepy. He dozed off into a sound sleep and Shom went away.

*

THE SECRET

"Good morning." A sweet, familiar voice woke Steve up from a really pleasant sleep. He opened his eyes to see little Pinkoo sitting on his nose and smiling at him.

"Good Morning, Pinkoo," murmured a sleepy Steve. "You are always at the right time, at the right place."

As he slowly got out of bed, he noticed a maroon colored gown, like the one all the monks were wearing, kept near his bed. "Is it for me?" he asked Pinkoo.

"Yes. Master wants you to wear it for the ceremony today," Pinkoo replied. "Now, get ready quickly. You have a long day ahead. Steve was looking forward to everything that was destined for him. He knew that in this house of God anything that comes to him would be a gift of the Lord.

In no time, he was bathed and dressed in his new gown. Pinkoo took him to the main hall of the Gompa. The whole place was filled with the mist that had entered from the main door. Behind the blue mist, the orange glow of the flickering lamps filled the atmosphere with serenity.

Pinkoo flew away to get Shom, while Steve stood there all alone. There was not a soul in the hall, and that made him feel a little lonely, and scared. Before he could dwell on that feeling, a figure appeared from behind the mist. It was Shom. Shom's kind smile elated his spirit. "Come, my child."

Shom guided Steve right up to the marble lotus. "We are here to seek the blessings of Lord Buddha," said Shom and picked up a medallion kept at the feet of the gold statue.

The medallion looked like a piece out of an antique shop. It was made of a strange alloy. There was a thousand-petal lotus embossed at the center of its pendant. Around the lotus were seven gems—each of a different color. Together, they were the seven colors of the rainbow. The chain of the medallion was made by combining seven cords—each of a different metal.

Shom put the chain around Steve's neck. "It looks beautiful on you, Steve. For ages, this medallion has been passed on from one generation of monks to the other. But only once in centuries comes a soul, who is worthy of wearing it. I was told this story by my Master, when I was your age. This medallion will safeguard all positive energies and ward off all negative forces. It will protect you. Keep it on you always; never lose it."

As the medallion was placed around his neck, Steve felt a sense of well-being pass through his body. He involuntarily bowed before Buddha's statue, even before Shom could say, "Now, thank Buddha for your good fortune, my child. Thank him for you have been granted the wonderful honor of wearing this."

"Come, let's go now," said Shom, after Steve was back on his feet. They walked out of the Gompa. There was a dense mist outside and it was still dark.

"Hold my hand" said Shom. Steve blindly followed Shom, as he was led through the mist. But, Shom did not even need to fumble his way through it. He knew every turn, climb and fall of the path to the Butterfly Nest.

On the way, Steve remembered the Trust Walk. Although he was not blindfolded, Steve was not able to see anything in the dark. But he was surrendered to Shom.

Once inside the dome, there was light all around. The green little florescent colored butterfly eggs were glowing like a multitude of twinkling stars on earth. Shom walked with Steve to the center of the dome and they sat on the floral bench. They were silent for a while. There was no sound inside the dome. Not even the sound of the fluttering of the wings of the butterflies, who were still asleep. After a while Steve heard a distant sound of a bird. Then, a few more birds starting chirping. Soon, the roof of the dome started moving. The butterflies were waking up too. Finally, Shom spoke.

"Hear the birds and butterflies, Steve? It's time for them to wake up to another morning. A morning that will be very different for you and me. With the first ray of the sun, a new chapter will open in our lives. This will lead to the fulfillment of our purpose on this earth...yours as well as mine."

Shom knew that Steve's young mind may not be able to completely comprehend what he was saying; so he added, "Don't worry, my boy. This experience will be the most beautiful and memorable experience of your life. Just be with me and do as I say."

Shom then looked up at the butterfly dome. All the butterflies were awake by then. They fluttered their wings and filled the Butterfly Nest with a soft breeze. Shom raised his hands toward them and addressed them. "O Blessed Friends! The time has come for us to visit the 'Secret' once again. So please make way."

Shom then held Steve's hand. "Stay on this bench, Steve, and do not move until I tell you."

The breeze created by the fluttering of the butterflies started getting stronger. Steve looked up and saw that the millions of butterflies that formed the dome had started to fly around in circles. Soon the entire dome started revolving. The butterfly breeze soon became a strong wind and before Steve could get a grip on what was happening, it turned into what could only be described as a tornado. Steve felt that he would be blown away. He held Shom's hand tightly and was visibly frightened. Shom clutched Steve's hand and said, "Don't panic, my child. God is taking care of us."

The tornado got stronger, and all the plants and the glittering butterfly eggs started rotating in its tow. Soon, the ground of the Butterfly Nest was revolving. The twinkling eggs were swept up; they created a multicolored mist all around. Everything seemed to be sucked toward the center of the tornado.

Steve and Shom were sitting on the floral bench, right there, at the center of the tornado. However, though everything around them was revolving fervently, their seat was steady.

As the tornado gathered an incredibly dizzying speed, Steve noticed a hole opening up, below their seat. The hole emanated bright light. Gradually, the hole grew bigger and the light became brighter. The bright beam reached the top of the dome and spread all over.

Steve could see the hole grow larger, at his feet. The radiance of the light was almost blinding. The tornado wind was so strong that he could feel his skin flapping against himself.

He looked at Shom who seemed to be unaffected by all that was happening around him. His eyes were closed, as in meditation. Steve closed his eyes out of fear. But then, he realized that his seat, which was steady until now, had started to move. Startled, he opened his eyes and was shocked to see the hole in the center of the ground had grown huge and his seat was floating over the hole.

The bright light had taken over the whole place. Everything, including the air and the essence of the Butterfly nest, was now sucked into the hole. Steve looked at Shom. His eyes were still closed. But his hands, which were still gripping Steve firmly, signaled Steve to remain calm.

Gradually, their floating floral bench was lowered into the hole. Steve saw the hole above them. It was now becoming smaller. The tornado slowed down and eventually stopped, and the hole closed above them. There was darkness all around. It was completely silent. Everything was still.

For a brief moment, Steve thought he heard a faint buzz near him, as if a fly was around him. Within seconds, the sound disappeared. However, it made Shom uneasy. "There is something unusual around here," he said. In the darkness he addressed someone. "Friends, can we quickly light up this place?"

A spot of tiny light appeared in the darkness. It seemed to come from far below. The light reached closer, followed by many such tiny lights. And then, hundreds of tiny spots of lights came floating in. They formed two rows that revealed a long staircase going down. Steve could not see what the staircase led to. As the lights reached closer, Steve discovered that they were glow worms. Their flickering lights lent a warm glow to the mystical staircase. Steve marveled at the unusual sight. He looked at Shom, who smiled back and said "Come Steve, let us start our journey into the heart of the Secret."

Steve looked down at the seemingly endless row of stone steps. He wondered how long he would have to walk to reach the end of the staircase. "Don't worry," said Shom "everything in this beautiful place is made for your comfort. Come, let's walk down." Shom held Steve's hand and stepped on the first step. To Steve's great surprise the stone staircase started to move down like an escalator.

"There, my child! Didn't I tell you that everything here is made for your comfort?" said Shom. "These steps were built many centuries back. Our civilization was far more advanced than today's scientific world."

The steps took them down a long vertical tunnel. Steve observed that the walls of the tunnels were engraved with various figures and forms.

"These murals etched on the walls, depict the history of our civilization," explained Shom. Steve was looking at the murals carefully when the figure of a warrior seemed to move. Steve felt like the warrior looked at him.

"Don't worry," said Shom holding Steve's hand. "These are guards who have safeguarded the Secret, for centuries."

Shom continued to explain the meaning of the paintings that they passed, until they reached the bottom of the staircase. In front of them was a wall of water, which was flowing from the bottom to the top. "What is the source of this waterfall? How come it is flowing against gravity? And where do we go now?"—these and several other questions were on Steve's mind. And as if to answer them, Shom raised his hand and pointed his finger to the center of the water wall. The wall parted into two, from the center, like curtains. Shom and Steve entered into the space that was formed in between. Once they were on the other side, the water curtains were pulled back to form the wall of flowing water.

Shom and Steve were now facing an inconceivable mirror maze. The entire space ahead of them was surrounded by unfathomable layers of mirrors. The ceilings and walls that enclosed the space comprised fixed as well suspended mirrors of different shapes and sizes. Even the floor had steps and platforms made of mirrors.

And in this mirror room, floating in mid-air were seven crystal globes that were revolving in fixed, interconnected orbits. After every few seconds, the globes would start glowing from the inside. Steve was fascinated by the crystal globes. He reached out to touch one of them. It stopped in its orbit and, as a result, the other six bumped into it. Within a moment all the crystal balls skid out of their orbit, dashing into one another. Steve was petrified. The crystal looked delicate. It seemed like the globed would shatter, any moment. He looked at Shom pleadingly. Shom rushed to stand between all the globes. He held both his hands in the position of an 'X.' Soon the crystals returned to their original orbits and started to revolve around Shom. He stepped back and looked at Steve who was nervous with guilt and fear. "Don't worry, my boy. These globes may look delicate but they are so strong that nothing can destroy them; not even a nuclear explosion. They are here for an important cause. I will explain that later."

Steve let out a heavy sigh and looked around. He saw that all the mirrors were moving in different directions. The walls and partitions were moving; the layers of ceiling were moving; and all the steps and platforms on the floor were moving. Steve was amazed to see thousands of his images appear and disappear all around him. He was lost in the mirror maze, when he realized that he could not see Shom's image in any mirror. He nervously looked around and saw that his Master was still standing beside him.

"Wondering which way to go?" asked Shom. Actually, Steve was wondering why he could not see Shom's reflection on any of the thousand mirrors!

"Well, you see that big mirror in the center of this room," continued Shom. There were thousands of mirrors in that room. "Which mirror is he referring to?" thought Steve.

"Look carefully, Steve," said Shom. "There is only one mirror in the center of this room that is not moving. See that one over there?" Steve finally located the only mirror that was not moving. Surprisingly, that was the only mirror in which he could see Shom's reflection. But he was shocked when he discovered that he could not see his "Don't get bothered by all that is happening around, my boy," said Shom. "That mirror is our doorway to the Secret. Come with me."

*

AN UNBELIEVABLE ENCOUNTER

Shom walked up to the mirror as Steve watched him, wondering if yet another door would open inside it. But something unexplainable happened. Shom walked right into the mirror and merged into his reflection. Steve stood there, first marveling at what happened; then wondering what he was to do next. His master had disappeared on the other side of the mirror. Now he was all alone inside the huge and mysterious miorror maze. He went up and touched the mirror into which Shom had disappeared. It felt solid, like any other mirror. He touched the mirror on all sides but could not find a passage to go to the other side. There was a strange stillness about the place inspite of the fact that every object in the mirror maze was in motion. Strangely enough all the movement did not create any sound what so ever. The silence was such that Steve could hear the sound of his breathing. He could even feel his heart, throb. Probably his heart was breathing faster because of his nervousness. For a few seconds the pin drop silence was broken by a buzzing sound that come and disappeared like lightening. Steve was not prepared for this shock. He got very scared and prayed that he would some how be with his grandmaster. And as if on cue, from inside the mirror Shom extended his hand toward Steve. "Come, my child," said Shom, "hold my hand and enter the Secret!" A little scared, Steve walked toward the mirror.

Suddenly, he heard that buzzing sound again. Was it the fly that he had felt earlier, when they'd come down through the tornado's center. It was an irritating buzz. Was it just his imagination? Steve stopped to shoo it, when Shom asked "What happened, Steve? What is bothering you?"

Steve forgot about the nagging fly and walked toward the mirror. He could see Shom's reflection in the mirror. But, Shom's arm was extending out of the mirror. For a moment, Steve stood still, amazed by what he was seeing.

"Come on Steve." There was a sense of urgency in Shom's voice. "We are getting late. We have to enter the Secret before the first ray of the sun reaches it." Steve held his Master's hand and simply walked into the mirror, as if there was nothing between him and the other end of the mirror. On the other side of the mirror, a different world was awaiting him. He turned around and stood still.

Steve felt like he had entered heaven. Before his eyes opened up the most impressive marvel of architecture he had ever imagined. A soft fragrance of sandalwood pervaded the majestic hall. Everything was made of sandalwood. On the front wall was an imposing sandalwood statue of Lord Buddha, sitting in a meditative posture. The statue was seated on a large lotus that had thousands of beautiful petals. It appeared so fresh, as if it had just bloomed. In front of the lotus on which Buddha was sitting, there were seven crystal balls. These looked exactly like the crystal balls in the mirror maze.

A beautiful lotus garden etched in sandalwood decorated the walls of the hall. On both sides of the hall, huge pillars that appeared to be made of white marble went up to the ceiling. But strangely, the pillars did not support the ceiling. They were about two feet under the ceiling.

"What was the point of having pillars that would not support the ceiling?" thought Steve. "May be, they were merely decorative." Steve was lost in the beauty and fragrance of the place, when he felt a gentle pat on his shoulder. He looked up to see Shom smiling at him.

"Like this place?" asked Shom.

"It's beautiful. And, so peaceful! But why is it called the 'Secret.' What is so secretive about this beautiful place?"

"That's exactly what I am going to tell you now," said Shom. "This is the place of God that protects the biggest 'Secret' on earth. And the 'Secret' is hidden in those crystal balls placed near the lotus at the feet of Lord Buddha. Centuries back, our ancestors made seven paintings, based on old scriptures that described the power of the Sun God. These paintings were placed in those seven crystal balls.

"Together, the seven paintings can be used to harness the power of the sun on earth. This immense power is equivalent to that of many nuclear bombs. A power beyond the imagination of the human mind. Anyone who acquires this power can conquer the world in no time. This power, if wrongly used, can destroy everything on earth. All life, all vegetation, the mountains, the seas, the forests—everything will perish, in a matter of seconds. Imagine what will happen if the sun were to collide with our earth? Our earth will never be the same. It will perish. Just a charred globe; reduced to ashes. But, on the other hand, this great powerhouse of infinite energy can also be used for the betterment of humanity. If this power is positively channelized, it will change the face of the earth. It can avert natural calamities like earthquakes, tornados and tsunami. Mass destruction and violence will stop forever, as no global power will dare to face this super power. This energy can conserve nature and bring back earth to its bountiful past."

Steve was listening in disbelief and amazement. Shom went on. "But in every age, it has happened thus: for every positive effort, there have been negative forces working against it. Down the centuries, evil powers of the black world have kept track of the 'Secret.' They've made every effort to acquire it. And for generations, we have tried to save it...which is why these paintings have been guarded so zealously."

"You have possessed this secret for centuries now." Steve asked, "Then why have you never used it?"

"You have asked the right question, at the right time, Steve," said Shom. "And, this is where 'You' come in my boy."

"Me?" wondered Steve. "How come? I know nothing about these paintings."

"Let me explain," said Shom. "You know that the white light of the sun, as our eyes see it, is actually made up of seven colors—the colors of the rainbow."

"Yes," said Steve, but not too confidently. He vaguely remembered Aunt Susan, at the orphanage, telling him about the seven colors that were part of light.

"VIBGYOR-Violet, Indigo, Blue, Green, Yellow, Orange and Red," reminded Shom. "These seven colors come together to make white. And, these seven colors are represented by the seven paintings. When these paintings come together, they create the supreme power—the white light of the sun."

Steve was intrigued, but he could still not understand his role in this scheme of things. "So, what do I do here?" he asked.

"You are the only human being who is born with the power to convert the ray of the sun into the seven colors of the rainbow. That is why you have the seven rainbow-like lines on your palm. That is why your body temperature shot up when you saw the rainbow from the mountains. And, that is why your warden, Mr. Arnold was thrown away, when he hit you on your right palm," Shom explained. "The seven lines on your palm have an immense power that you are not aware of. These mystic lines will help to ignite the latent energy in these paintings. One by one, these seven paintings will bring to life seven creatures, each bearing one rainbow color. And then the 'Seven Creatures of the Rainbow' will merge together to create the supreme power—the Son of the Sun!"

At this point, Shom bent down and held Steve with both his hands. "My child, we have waited for generations for you to come to earth." After saying this, Shom's face changed a bit. Steve thought he saw an expression concern, as Shom turned away and said, "But, there is a missing link in all this. I think I should explain this better, now. When our ancestors first succeeded in creating these paintings, they were fortunate to find a boy like you, who had the powers to energize the paintings. But before the Creatures of the Rainbow could come to life, the boy was kidnapped by evil forces."

"Our ancestors fought hard and rescued six of the seven paintings, but could not rescue the boy. Without him, we could do nothing. And, we still have no clue about the where the seventh painting is. But, for generations, we have safeguarded the six remaining paintings. These are in six of the seven globes you see here. And for all these generations, we have waited for you to arrive, my child. Now you are here. It's time for a great change on earth."

Shom held Steve's hand and walked toward Buddha. He bowed before the statue. Then, looking upward, he closed his eyes and waved his hands above his head. Sparks, like fireworks, came out of his fingers. The sparks flew across the hall and struck the top of the large pillars in the hall. That's when Steve realized that the pillars were actually huge candles. The sparks from Shom's hands lit those candles. In the glow of that warm light, a third eye appeared on the forehead of Buddha's statue. The eye opened and emitted a beam of light that fell on Steve and Shom, like a spotlight.

"Hold my hand, Steve, and look at Buddha's third eye," said Shom. "Right now, all the members of the Gompa can see us."

Outside the monastery, every member was gathered in the courtyard. The sun was about to rise. In the orange-golden sky, the monks saw Shom and Steve, as if figures on a movie screen. Everyone bowed down to Shom, as they heard his voice floating from his image in the sky.

"My fellow monks! Today is a day that we have waited for, for centuries. In a few moments from now, we will present the 'Secret' to you. And this is possible because we have in our midst the most precious link. Without him, we would have never seen this day. And this valuable link, this messanger of good fortune is young 'Steve!'"

Everyone hailed Steve.

Shom continued, "As I said, Steve is most precious to us. We shall therefore vow to protect him, even at the cost of our lives. We are about to begin a new chapter in our lives. We cannot be sure how things will change. But, whatever the outcome, always remember to protect Steve! May God be with us!" As Shom spoke these last words, Shom's and Steve's images disappeared from the sky. Everyone bowed down.

Down in the Secret chamber, Shom gave some final instructions to Steve. "Now listen carefully, my boy! We are going straight ahead to experience something great and marvelous. So far, it's been going according to what we have planned...except, we don't have the seventh painting. But, that should not be a problem. When the six creatures are formed from the paintings that we do have, they will attract their seventh companion, from anywhere on this globe."

Shom held Steve close to him and continued, "Just remember! Once the paintings come out of their crystal balls, they cannot reenter them. If anything goes wrong, the only way to protect these paintings is to go to the mirror maze and put them into the crystal balls of that room. Then, the crystal balls will travel to seven preprogrammed destinations, in different parts of the world. God is with us. He will take care of everything."

Shom led Steve to the center of the room, where the floor was painted with the image of shining sun.

"Do you see that small vent in the wall, above the head of Lord Buddha?" asked Shom. Steve nodded. "In less than a minute, the first ray of the sun will enter this room, through that vent."

"Now, raise your right hand, son."

Steve obeyed. Then, Shom explained, "When the sun's ray enters, it will hit your raised hand. You need to stand still, right here. Don't get disturbed; just observe what's happening. Bless you, my child. May

Buddha be with you!"

Shom's words were assuring. But, Steve could feel his heartbeat increasing steadily. He stood still, with his hand raised, waiting for the first ray of the sun to touch his palm. There was stillness all around. The wax from the huge candles had slowly started melting. The patterns created by the molten wax added to the mystical ambience.

Steve looked at Shom, whose eyes were closed. He was calmly chanting some mantras. Then with a click, the lid of the vent opened. It brought in a whiff of mist into the room. And finally, piercing through the mist, came the first golden ray of the morning sun. It traveled straight to Steve's palm and seemed to dissolve into him. Steve had never experienced this sensation before. He could feel the rays of the sun traveling through every vein in his body. He could feel every cell of his being absorbing the rays and coming alive. Steve could see his body glow with a golden light.

Then, he could feel something moving on his raised palm. It was the rainbow lines pulsating with life. Each line dazzled with a different color of the rainbow.

First, a violet ray was emitted from Steve's palm and spread around a beautiful violet hue. Then, a soft indigo ray traveled beside the violet ray. This was followed by a blue ray and then the green, yellow, and orange rays; and finally the red completed the rainbow. It was the most magical rainbow Steve had seen. Each ray was alive with sparkling stars of the same color traveling across the path of the rainbow.

Steve was mesmerized. He was lost in the glitter of the colors. All he could see was the magical rainbow; and all he could hear was his Master's elevating chanting.

"Steve." Shom's calm call broke the trance.

Steve had almost forgotten his Master's presence in the room. He turned his head to hear Shom caution him. "Do not move, my child. Just listen carefully and do exactly as I say."

With complete attention, Steve followed Shom's instructions. "Keep your palm upright; but slowly lower your hand. Move it down, until your hand is at the same level as Lord Buddha's feet."

Steve saw that as he lowered his hand, the rainbow moved from the head of Buddha, down his body to his feet. In this process, the statue itself got transformed. Just above Buddha's head, a violet halo appeared. The halo then morphed into a beautiful lotus with a thousand petals. Then, Buddha's forehead glowed with an indigo hue. And all the other colors of the rainbow traveled down his body. The wonderful sandalwood statue of Buddha appeared to have come to life.

"Well done, Steve," encouraged Shom. "Now, point your rainbow toward the seven globes kept at Buddha's feet."

Steve lowered his hand further. The rainbow traveled with his hand and as it reached the crystal globes, it branched into its seven colors—each color touching one of the seven crystal globes. Each globe absorbed its color and started glowing with that color. Then, each globe started opening up, until it was split into two halves. Very old-looking paper pieces, rolled up like scrolls, popped out of six of the split globes and started floating mid-air.

All this while, Shom was chanting. When the paintings were out and floating, he said, "Steve, now you need to focus your rainbow on the floating scrolls."

Steve followed the instructions, as if in a hypnotic spell. He raised his palm again, until the colors of the rainbow touched the floating scrolls. As soon as the colored rays touched them, the scrolls unfurled. Six intricate paintings were revealed.

These paintings were not made on paper. The scrolls were made of the thin bark of some tree. The color of the bark had dulled. But, paintings on it had not blurred. The ink and the colors still looked fresh; especially the gold, silver and copper paints, which gave a unique shine to the paintings. The paintings did not have any discernible figures. There were geometrical figures and scriptures, arranged in some kind of pattern. When the rays of the rainbow touched them, the scriptures and geometrical patterns on each painting started moving. Their movement picked on a dizzying speed and they seemed to merge into one another and take a form. Each painting began to absorb the color of the ray falling on it.

Steve could was now feel the strain of keeping his hand in the same position for all this while. He was beginning to lose his concentration. But then, he was struck by what was happening in the paintings. By now the paintings were completely soaked in their respective colors; and Steve thought he could see little liquid droplets of those colors oozing out of the paintings. Yes! The patterns and scriptures on each painting had merged into one another and were now morphing into drops of colored gel. These drops came together and started taking form.

Steve's attention was caught by the violet painting, as its liquid gel took the form of a wondrous creature. Its body was like two wobbly round lumps of colored jelly—one on top of the other. The smaller jelly lump on top was like the face a new born baby with large innocent eyes.

There was constant movement within the transparent jelly body that glowed from within. It was jutting out of the painting, but was still fixed to it. Steve watched in awe, while that being looked down on itself and pushed a pair of hands and feet, out of its jelly body. There was a shy smile on its face as it looked up and pulled the hands and feet back into its body.

Steve's eyes moved to the five other paintings and found that similar creatures had emerged from them. All six creatures jumped from their paintings into the crystal globe below them.

Lost in awe of the 'Creatures of the Rainbow,' Steve had forgotten about his raised hand, until he heard Shom's voice. "You can lower your arm, Steve. See and enjoy God's wonderful creations."

"I love them, Master," Steve said; then added excitedly, "Can I touch them?"

"Not now, my child," said Shom. "Right now, we are just one step away from the great realization. If only we had the seventh painting, the group would be complete and we could create the most powerful creature in the world, the Son of the Sun! But, we will have to wait for our six little friends to find out their seventh brother. And then, our journey will be complete."

"Your journey shall not stop, my friends! I have come to gift you the missing link in your journey." A deep, hoarse voice boomed from behind him, shattering the tranquility of the moment.

*

THE INTRUDER

In a moment, everything seemed to change rapidly. Steve saw fear in the large, innocent-looking eyes of those little creatures, as they jumped back into their paintings. They soon took the form of tiny droplets of colored gel. The droplets seemed to get soaked into the paintings. They merged into the color of the age old paintings and disappeared.

Shom and Steve turned, in shock, to see a striking tall, lean figure behind them. There was something completely evil about this man. It was as if this intruder's persona exuded something that instilled fear in anyone who saw him. His long face had a pointed nose and thin lips that were painted white. Under his shaven eyebrows were big drugged-looking eyes, with thick bushy lashes. The steep forehead was painted red. And on the head was thick, long hair, knotted at its end. Above his head hovered a bunch of bats, flying in circles to create a black halo. A long thick beard had grown down, all the way to his knees. He wore a long and flowing black gown and a garland of human baby skulls over it. There were dazzling rubies pierced into his earlobes. In his right hand, he held an ivory shaft that had the figure of two golden mating snakes and a big diamond on top.

Steve was immediately reminded of the menacing bats that had followed him all this while. Petrified, he stood there, trembling. Shom sensed Steve's fear and drew him closer.

Shom himself sounded uneasy and confused as he confronted the man. "Who are you? And how could you set foot into this protected abode of God?"

"Shom, my friend!" said the intruder in a voice that seemed to come from a deep tunnel.

Steve looked up to see that Shom was also shocked that the man knew his name!

The intruder continued, "To answer your first question, my name is Kapaal Baba. People call me Kapaal because I worship God through sacrifice of living objects. And 'Baba', because people respect and fear me…rightfully so." Kapaal's proud, resounding voice sent a chill down Steve's spine. "And your second question—how I entered this fiercely guarded place? The answer's simple." Kapaal snapped his fingers, saying "Like this!" and disappeared

Steve and Shom grew more uncomfortable, wondering where Kapaal could have gone. Just then, Steve heard the same buzzing sound that was bothering him when he entered the Secret. The next moment, a small fly with a red head was flying right in front of his nose. Steve clenched his Master's hand tightly and tried to hide behind his robes.

"Remember the fly that was following you all the

way into the Secret, Steve? Would Shom ever allow me into this place, otherwise?" Both Steve and Shom were shocked at this revelation. Kapaal went on. "And dear Steve, I hope you have not forgotten how my cute little bats kept track of you at every step. Remember? You must be in love with them by now." said the fly and took Kapaal's form again. Steve hated every word Kapaal had uttered.

"That answers your second question Shom" said Kapaal.

Shom had not finished. "So, why are you..."

Kapaal interrupted Shom with, "No, no, no, my friend! Kapaal does not answer more than two questions at a time. Now, it's my turn to ask a question." Kapaal took a pause to watch their reaction.

And this was the question. "What will make you really, really happy right now?"

"To see you out of this sacred place, right away." For the first time since he met him, Steve sensed anger in Shom's voice.

"Wrong answer!" said Kapaal with a scornful smile. "What will really make you happy is...THIS!" And he drew out a scroll from the sleeve of his long gown. A scroll that looked much like the six painting scrolls Steve had seen earlier.

"Now tell me honestly. Doesn't this painting make you really happy?" Kapaal grinned, showing off all his yellowed teeth. "This, my friend, is your missing link. The seventh painting, the one that would create the seventh Creature of the Rainbow—the Red creature. For ages, your monastery has protected the six paintings of the Rainbow. My poor ancestors could lay their hands on only one painting. However, they were kind enough to safeguard this one hell-of-a-valuable painting. And I am now the proud owner who possesses this invaluable work of art. Now, isn't that something to be really proud of?" saying this, Kapaal kissed the painting.

"Please come to the point, now," said Shom. "What exactly do you want?"

"I want a share of exactly what you want. A share of the supreme power, which can conquer the world!" Kapaal smiled. "Look Shom, my friend. Let me make things easy for you. This one painting can complete the creation of the super power! Imagine, my friend, the things we can do with this power."

"All nations, whether rich with oil or money; they will all bow before us. Nuclear plants will be like little rats when they face our power. Together, we can rule from any corner of the world. These mountains or some beach if you like. You won't even need your monastery monks to boss over Shom." Kapaal went on wickedly.

"Or, would you rather be happy with six of your slimy cute creatures and play ping pong with them for the rest of your life? The choice is yours, my friend!"

Shom kept quiet for a while. It was clear to Steve that Shom did not want to be party to anything with that evil man. But, Kapaal was not really looking for agreement. His plan was well worked out.

"Don't worry, Shom. If you do not agree to join hands with me, I have another option for you." Saying this he handed over the painting to the bats that were hovering around his head. The bats flew with it to the top of the burning candles. "A 'No' from you and the last painting will be turned into ash, in minutes. The choice is yours, my friend."

"Stop it!" shouted Shom. "Bring back the painting and place it where it belongs—at Lord Buddha's holy feet."

"So be it!" announced Kapaal. "My little 'Black Beauties' bring down the painting." The bats obeyed their master. Kapaal took the painting and gave it to Shom. Shom took it solemnly, walked silently to the altar, and placed the painting at the feet of Buddha. He then turned toward Kapaal.

"We are ready for the great moment!" he said to Kapaal. "As you understand, the whole process is very precarious. We can't take any risk and can't have any movements in this room. So may I request you to ask your bats to stop hovering over your head?"

Kapaal readily agreed. He snapped his fingers and the bats settled down—some on his shoulders, some on his hands.

When the fluttering of the bats was over, Shom closed his eyes to meditate. But, suddenly he heard a shriek.

"Aaargh..." Kapaal was shouting, "You thirsty blood sucker! Can't you have patience? Wait! I'll fill your tummies when all this is done." Then, Kapaal turned to Shom. "See? This is why I don't let those vampire bats cling to me. They are always thirsty for blood. Naughty boys! Really sorry for the interruption, my friend." He then moved aside and stood near one of the giant candles and said, "I won't come in the way of your rituals, Shom. You may now continue your great work. I'll just stand here and wait for the power and riches that we and our ancestors have always dreamt for."

"His dreams are filled with greed and hatred," Steve heard Shom saying; but like during the initiation rituals, his lips were not moving. Kapaal could not hear Shom, or so it seemed; because he just stood there grinning away at them.

Shom took Steve's hand and motioned him to turn toward the statue.

Then, Shom continued to say to Steve, without speaking, "If these paintings and the super power were to come in possession of this wicked Kapaal, he will destroy the world."

"It is the Lord's kind wish that after ages this seventh painting should come to his lotus feet. Pray with me Steve, that we may protect the power from going into wrong hands. Let's ask him to guide us that we may be able to hide this power away from these evil eyes."

Shom stood motionless for a while, with his eyes closed, hands folded in front of him, in prayer. Finally, he opened his eyes and smiled at the statue of Buddha. He looked pleased. With gratitude, he bowed before the statue and stood facing the sunrays coming in from the vent. His body was absorbing the rays and glowing like the sun. Shom raised his hands, which now seemed to be emitting the light that his body was soaking up. From the tip of his fingers burst out hundreds of delicate rays that looked like the first rays of the morning sun. Gradually he started to clench his fist. As the pressure on his fist grew, the rays became bigger and stronger. Just as the heat of the sun grows through the day, the rays of his fist became brilliant and stared emitting the heat of the mid day sun.

Suddenly, Shom turned his fist and the blinding rays towards the giant candle under which Kapaal was standing. In a matter of seconds, the entire candle was melting. Before Kapaal could know it, wax was falling all over him and his legs were completely dug in molten wax.

"What have you done, you traitor? I trusted you, and..." he shouted as he struggled to lift his legs. The wax poured on him, relentlessly. His 'Black Beauty' bats tried flying off, but their wings were stuck. They let out shrieks that pierced every bit of that place.

"You have made a grave mistake Shom!" Kapaal shouted at the top of his voice, while he was already waist-deep in wax. "You have no idea of what I can do! You underestimate my powers, Shom."

"Your powers can never be greater than the powers of the Lord," said Shom calmly, as the strong rays from his fist kept melting the wax pillar at an alarmingly fast pace. "These paintings are sacred and Lord Buddha will never allow them to be with a greedy man like you. You want to use the Power for your own greed, at the cost of enslaving humanity. So remain buried here, at the feet of God, until your heart is clear and your intentions are right. I will pray for you."

Shom went on melting the wax with his powerful

rays, without a pause. By now, Kapaal's body was completely submerged under the molten wax. Only his head could be seen; but he didn't stop trying to wriggle out. And, he did not stop his threats. "I warn you, Shom. This wax or, for that matter, any substance on this earth can never confine Kapaal for long. You will repent this, Shom. Kapaal is born to rule the world. The universe shall bow down at my feet one day. And you shall perish under my powers. I promise you that."

Kapaal's death-like yell resounded in that place. He opened his mouth and took a big, long breath, as he seemed to gather all his energy. His eyes became red and fierce. He then opened his mouth and blew out a storm of flames. Like thunderbolt, the fire from his mouth hit all the other candles. The flames of the candles got bigger, starting to look like monstrous bonfires. As the flames increased, the candles started melting down. Soon, the entire floor was covered with wax.

Kapaal's mouth, ears, and eyes were all covered with wax. With the last of his breaths he spit fire and shouted, "Now you are doomed, Shom; and so is that nitwit kid. This is the molten grave for those paintings too. Die a painful death. We will definitely meet in our rebirth. Farewell!" With these last words Kapaal and his bats were completely buried under the wax.

Shom had to act fast now. All the candles were melting rapidly. Shom rushed to the altar and picked up all the seven paintings. He took one last look at Buddha and bowed at his feet. He then turned to

Steve; but Steve was not in his place. For a second, Shom stood motionless with fear. He looked around and called out frantically. "Steve, my child, where are you?" There was no response. The boy was most precious for him. "Where are you, Steve? Answer me, my boy!"

*

NO WAY OUT

Tons of melting wax and flaming candle was causing huge crackling sounds. There was a faint sound amidst all the noise. "Speak up, Steve. I can feel your presence in this room. Speak up, child!" Shom was getting desperate as the molten wax was rising. Suddenly a giant candle fell and created a huge wave in the sea of wax. Shom's feet got submerged under the wax. He was taken by surprise and knew now that he could float no more. He did not bother about himself and called out for Steve as loud as he could. "Do not panic, my child. Your Master will save you. Just call out, Steve!"

"Master!" Steve's faint voice was heard amidst the chaotic noise. "Steve! My child." Shom reacted immediately.

The wax was up to Shom's knees; but he did not seem to care about his pain. "I can hear you, my boy! Where are you?" Shom called out aloud.

"I am here, Master!" Shom heard Steve's voice from behind a giant candle. He picked up all his strength and moved in the direction of the voice. He had to struggle hard as the wax was rising and burning every inch of skin that it touched.

He just went on in the direction of the candle, the paintings clutched tightly in his hands. As he approached the candle, he spotted Steve and was relieved to see that he was standing on a table.

"Ah...my child! Thank God you are safe." Shom hurriedly picked up Steve in his lap. "We must get out of this place right now, Steve!"

Shom rushed through the burning lava-like wax, which had come up to his waist. Steve could see great pain in Shom's eyes. But Shom wouldn't relent and kept wading, making sure that Steve and the paintings were above the wax.

"Help me, my Lord," prayed Shom. "Help me reach the mirror maze."

With all the vigor he could garner from within, Shom rushed toward the entrance of the mirror maze. The candles were melting faster now. Two more of those towering candles fell into the molten wax creating a huge ripple. As a result a series of waves was created in the sea of wax. The waves came together, rose up to the ceiling, and traveled toward Shom. Shom sensed the danger and with all his might leapt toward the entrance of the mirror maze, pleading in prayer. "Help, Lord Buddha. Help!" He stretched to touch the huge mirror at the entrance of the maze and within a fraction of a second they got sucked into the mirror maze. The huge wave of molten wax lashed against the huge mirror which remained unaffected by its impact. The boiling lava of wax was fast filling the entire hall.

Inside the mirror maze everything was tranquil and silent, as if nothing had happened. Shom looked around to ensure that everything was safe. Nothing had been touched in the mirror maze. It was cool inside, totally unaffected by the boiling temperature of the adjecent room. The mirrors were intact and moving in their position. The seven crystal globes were rotating in their axes. Having ensured that they were safe, Shom lowered Steve on to the floor.

"Thank the Lord that he did not let you be harmed," Shom said to Steve. "We have very little time left. First, we have to secure these paintings and take you to a safe place. Let's hasten to the crystal globes."

Shom was trying to move when he realized that his feet were stuck. The molten wax was solidifying on his body and glueing him to the ground. Soon all the wax would dry and set him to the floor. Shom took in a deep breath and closed his eyes. With a ripping sound, the skin of his feet came off, as he lifted his feet, in one strong motion. The peeled skin stuck to the wax on the floor as Shom staggered forward.

Steve looked away from the gory sight. Shom did not even wince. "Hold my hand Steve, and take me to the crystal globes."

Steve took him to the center of the mirror maze where the seven crystal globes were rotating. Shom could not stand on his feet any longer. He went down on his knees and handed over the paintings to Steve saying, "Now listen to me carefully, my boy. One by one, place the paintings on each of the seven globes.

"Remember to place them in order, from Violet to Red." Steve followed Shom's instructions. As soon as the seven paintings were on their respective crystal globes, the paintings disappeared into the globes. Each globe started glowing with the color of the painting. Shom looked at the globes with contentment.

"These paintings will not be secure in this place," he said in a weak voice. "Soon, they will start their journey to seven corners of the world. Only you will be able to locate them."

Shom closed his eyes, folded his hands in prayer, and started chanting. As the chanting continued, the globes started rotating faster. The intensity of the chanting increased and the rotation of the crystal globes increased. When the chanting reached a crescendo, the globes were rotating at such speeds that they looked blurred. And, before Steve could realize, the globes had vanished.

Shom collapsed on the ground, while Steve looked around helplessly.

On the other side of the mirror maze, the hall from which they came looked like the site of a volcanic eruption. Half the room was filled with molten wax, boiling like lava. The heat was tremendous and it was destroying everything around. The walls and the sandalwood carvings were charred. The beautiful sandalwood furniture had turned into ash. Most of the giant candles had melted and the rest would soon melt to fill the room completely with wax. The only thing that remained unaffected was the sandalwood statue of Buddha.

Suddenly, there appeared a stirring in the wax, somewhere in the center of the room. It looked like a whirlpool, which gradually grew in size. Soon, from the center of the whirlpool appeared a dazzling diamond. The diamond—it glistened like the sun as it came up. Then, attached to the shining diamond came out the face of two golden snakes. The golden snakes glistened in the brilliance of the bright light all around and revealed the magical shaft of Kapaal. And as the whirlpool grew deeper, out came Kapaal's hand, holding the shaft. And the next moment, everything changed.

A blast of ice and snow flakes burst out of the diamond and launched into the room. The freezing snow collided with the fire and molten wax. There was thick smoke all over. Nothing was visible except the glistening diamond and the glowing golden shaft. Thunder, lightning, and heavy snowing spread across the room, as the heat and fire started to die down. In a few moments, the wax was frozen solid. For a while, everything was still. And, then the room started shaking, as if struck by an earthquake.

The tremors reached the mirror maze as well. Shom, was unconscious so far, opened his weak eyes. He staggered up on his feet. The solid layers of wax were clinging to this burnt body. He stood up with great difficulty and looked around. The crystal globes were gone. Steve was in a state of shock. The tremor in the mirror maze grew in intensity.

"Come to me, Steve," said Shom in a feeble voice.

Steve was too shocked to move.

"Come to me quickly, my child. We have no time to lose." Shom's energy was dwindling fast.

The tremors grew. The moving mirrors stopped in their path. The glass floor started shaking. Steve could not gather the courage to move.

"Don't just stand there, Steve." Shom's voice was weak but firm. "Come to me, immediately."

"Yes Master," Steve obeyed. But as soon as he tried to move, he fell with the force of the tremor.

"Be brave, Steve," said Shom. "Get back on your feet and come to me."

Steve was willing to do anything that his Master asked him to; even if he had to battle with fear. He walked, fell, crawled, and finally managed to reach Shom.

Shom held Steve's shoulder and leaned on him. "Pay attention to every word that I am saying. The crystal globes have carried the paintings outside this place. They will travel on a fixed path and hide in seven different parts of the world. They will be hidden in secret places where no one can find them. No one but you!" Suddenly the floor shook so hard that Shom lost balance and fell on his knees.

"Help me, O Lord!" Shom pleaded in pain.

He held Steve's hand and said, "Help me stand up, my child." As he struggled to stand up, he continued, "I sense danger, Steve. You need to act quickly. There is a map that shows the way to the seven destinations of the paintings. The map lies in the Valley of Flowers. To be able to trace that map, you first need to find a secret scroll that is kept under the seat of Lord Buddha's statue, in the hall, where you enter our Gompa. Take that scroll to the Valley of Flowers, and..."

Before Shom could complete his sentence, there was a big blast in the hall that completely shook the mirror maze.

The rock solid wax in the adjacent hall started developing cracks, because of the impact of the blast inside it. The cracks grew bigger and wider, as the whole place shook violently. The huge mass of wax seemed to fall apart. Within minutes, there was another blast. The solid lumps of wax went flying across the room. And from inside the wax, burst out the vampire bats, and finally emerged Kapaal. It seemed as if the fire and molten wax had no impact on his body. His vampire bats were also unaffected. Boiling with rage, Kapaal dashed toward the mirror maze.

Inside the mirror maze, Shom apprehended the approaching danger. "Steve, its time for you to leave this place."

"No Master! I will not go without you," pleaded Steve.

"Steve, this place has to be vacated immediately. I am not able to walk. Your life is precious, my child. And remember, the sacred medallion. It will always protect you. Never lose it. Now, leave this place before something happens to you." Shom insisted.

"I can't leave you like this," said Steve adamantly.

"I command you to go, right now!" Shom raised his voice.

Just then, there was a blast at the door of the mirror maze. A huge ball of ice gushed into the mirror maze breaking open the door. In came Kapaal and screamed at the top of his voice. "No one goes out of this place! Now listen, you betrayer, I have not come here for child's play. After what you did to me, if you are still alive, it's because I have still not laid my hands on this boy or the paintings. Before things get worse, hand over the paintings and this boy to me."

"The paintings and the boy are sacred. And sacred things do not go to the evil," said Shom sternly. "Your evil intentions have brought you to this holy place. But you can never go out of here. As for Steve, he is God's child and will find a safe passage out of here." Shom turned and said, "Steve, leave this moment."

Steve started moving toward the water screen that was at the entrance of the mirror maze. But a furious Kapaal ordered "Steve! If you move another inch, I will destroy you."

Steve stopped in panic, but Shom insisted, "Go, Steve. Run! This evil man cannot stop you. Lord Budhha is with you."

Steve ran toward the water screen, as Kapaal lifted his shaft in rage. A sharp beam of ice blasted out of the shaft and traveled toward Steve. Shom knew instantly that if the lethal beam were to hit Steve, it could be fatal for the kid. In spite of being grounded, he used his entire last bit of strength and jumped to save Steve from the ice attack. With a blast, the ice beam struck Shom.

Steve turned to see what the loud sound was. He saw that Shom was standing between Kapaal and himself. Shom's feet were frozen, as if struck by snow. Shom turned toward Steve and pointed his finger at the water screen, which split. Steve ran up the stairs, and the water screen closed behind him.

Kapaal tried to aim another ray of ice at Steve. It struck the water screen, which now became a wall of ice.

As he continued up the staircase, Steve could hear blasts against this ice wall. Steve turned to find that the wall was growing thicker and would not relent.

From the other side of the ice wall, Steve could hear Kapaal raging in frustration. "Nothing has ever stopped Kapaal. Nothing can ever stop me from getting what I want...least of all, you, Shom. I had promised you death. And death you shall get."

Steve felt an immense sense of sadness gripping him as he heard Shom's feeble voice—a voice that he could hear more in his heart than in his ears. "Life and death is only in the hand of the Almighty. No human being has this power. As for you, Kapaal, you have sinned and God will punish you," said Shom calmly.

"Enough of your sermons!" shouted Kapaal. "With your legs frozen to the ground, how dare you speak to me? Your end is near, Shom. Now prepare to die!"

Steve had reached the end of the staircase, by this time.

In the mirror maze, below, Kapaal was pointing

his shaft at Shom. Before Kapaal could act, Shom waved his hands in the air. Millions of stars sparked out his fingers and hit all the mirrors in the maze. The mirrors swung toward Kapaal and formed a multi-layered glass cage around him. The impact of the mirrors was so hard that his shaft fell out of his hands. The mirror cage squeezed at him from all directions. He could not move an inch.

Before the attack of the mirrors, a vampire bat had managed to fly away. They escaped through the vent behind Lord Buddha's statue, in the hall.

Everything was absolutely still!

Steve managed to come out of the Secret passage. Exhausted and confounded by everything, he staggered through the Butterfly Nest, came up to the courtyard of the monastery, and fainted. There was total darkness before his eyes.

*

THE SEARCH BEGINS

Inside a deep, dark tunnel emerges a small beam of light. It is seen at a distance. The light grows stronger as it comes closer. The beam enlarges and spreads through the darkness, as the black fades into white. The white light becomes brighter and brighter until the darkness totally dissolves in it. Now there is white light everywhere. Gradually, the light turns into snow. And the snow grows. Heaps and heaps of snow that starts turning into ice cubes. The ice cubes multiply from hundreds to thousands to millions, until they become huge blocks of ice. Then, the ice blocks start growing, and become a wall of ice. And the wall grows bigger and stronger. It seems impenetrable. But a sharp ray penetrates it from the other end. The ray is very bright. It keeps drilling deep into the wall of ice. Slowly, cracks develop on the wall. The cracks widen as the beam continues to pierce the ice wall. Finally, the wall gives way. A huge blast shatters the wall into tiny crystals of ice. With the explosion, a blast of molten wax spreads all over...

Steve woke up with a jolt. His eyes tried to adjust to the rays of the morning sun that fell right on his face. He looked around. Everything seemed misty and hazy. He could make out that he was in a room where everything was white. He was lying on a white block of marble, covered with a white bed sheet. The only source of light was a small vent from where the golden rays were diffusing into the mist in the room. The sunrays and the fragrant mist were soothing Steve's frightened and tired mind. It felt like he was waking up from a horrible nightmare. He looked to his left and saw a big marble statue of Buddha lying beside him. The imposing statue scared him and he was about to scurry to his feet, when he heard a voice. "Take it easy, Steve. You are safe here, in God's house."

Steve recognized the face, as the monk came closer. He was Vyoma, a senior monk who was second in command, after Grandmaster Shom.

Vyoma smiled at Steve and affectionately caressed his hair. "How are you feeling now?"

"Don't know," was Steve's answer. "I am feeling kind of lost and exhausted."

"I can understand, Steve," said Vyoma. "You had a tough time. But God is kind; you are safe."

"How is Master? Is he...?" Steve could not complete the questions, as tears rolled down his cheek.

"Our Master is safe," assured Vyoma.

"How do you know?" asked Steve.

"He communicates with us from where he is now," replied Vyoma. "Right now, he is where you had seen him last—inside the mirror maze. He is stuck with the evil Kapaal. He will have to remain there. Else, Kapaal will escape. But, you don't worry, child. Our Master will always be safe because Lord Buddha is taking care of him."

"But how do we take him out of that place?" Steve was not satisfied with Vyoma's reassurance. "Master would be hungry, thirsty, and in pain!" Steve winced as he remembered Shom's burnt leg, with its skin peeled off.

"No Steve!" said Vyoma. "Our Master is beyond hunger, thirst, or pain. He is in the service of our Lord; and the Lord will take care of him."

"Why don't we all go there, together? We could capture Kapaal and save our Master." Steve was desperate.

Vyoma was amused by the boy's innocent insistence on helping his Master. "It's not that easy, Steve. Right now, our first concern is to find all the seven paintings from different parts of the world. Remember, Master told you about it, before you escaped. Master told me that only you can go on this mission; no one else can touch those paintings. We will support you in every way possible. But it's your journey, my child."

Steve fell silent for a while, wondering how he could fulfill this big an expectation.

"Don't worry, my boy." said Vyoma, as if reading his thoughts. "The longest journey starts with a single step. Have faith in God. Don't brood over it right now, because you are in great company. See who is here!"

Cheeka, who was waiting outside the room, came in flaunting his wrinkly-eyed smile. Steve and Cheeka hugged like they'd met after years of separation.

"I'm so glad to see you, Cheeka," said Steve.

"Me too!" said Cheeka, smiling at him.

"Someone else is glad too, Steve!" It was that tiny, familiar voice, again.

Steve smiled. "Pinkoo! Where are you?"

"As always...I am here!" Pinkoo said playfully.

Steve knew where to look for Pinkoo. He turned to his right shoulder, and there she was. Pinkoo fluttered her wings and sat on Steve's nose. "How is my 'best friend' feeling now?" she asked.

"Now that you are here, I am absolutely fine. But when I went to the..." Steve stopped midway, not sure of how much he could tell his friends.

Vyoma sensed Steve's dilemma. "It's okay, Steve. You can share all you want with them. Master wishes that you have them as your confidantes. But don't stress yourself right away."

Vyoma was about to leave the room, when Steve interjected, "Master told me about a secret scroll which is kept under the seat of Buddha, in the hall. I need to find that scroll."

"Yes Steve," said Vyoma, "but you need another day's rest. Relax and enjoy with your friends. We will start afresh tomorrow."

Steve spent the day with Cheeka, Pinkoo, and other friends in the monastery. They went to the hot-water fall and bathed for long. The hot water and the fresh air washed away all his pain.

Steve shared the incident at the Secret with Cheeka and Pinkoo. "Master risked his life to save me and the paintings." said Steve. "Now these seven paintings are hidden in seven secret places of the world. Master said that there is a map in the Valley of Flowers. This map will lead us to the hidden destinations. Have you seen the Valley of Flowers?"

"Yes of course," said Pinkoo excitedly. "All the butterflies from the Butterfly Nest go to the Valley of Flowers to collect their nectar. But I haven't seen any map there!"

"You're right; I don't remember seeing any map there!" said Cheeka, a bit confused.

"We will go there tomorrow," said Steve. "But I need to carry the Secret scroll to the Valley of Flowers. Cheeka and Pinkoo, will you come with me?"

"Of course," was the chorus, "first thing tomorrow morning!"

It was still dark and misty outside, as Vyoma guided Steve, Cheeka, and Pinkoo to the entrance hall. Behind the mountains, the sky was gradually getting brighter. Birds had started chirping. The group walked in silence. Steve noticed that Vyoma was carrying a big magnifying glass attached to a long silver stick. They entered the hall in silence. Like every time that he'd been there before, Steve was filled with a deep sense of peace and tranquility.

The incense sticks that were always burning, in the hall, were emanating smoky whiffs. Long flowing white curtains that covered the statue of Buddha appeared mysterious, as they swayed without any breeze. Vyoma took the children across the hall, up to the marble lotus. Vyoma touched his forehead to the white lotus and its petals opened revealing the holy water within it. They applied the water on their eyes.

The white curtains had moved aside to reveal the serene statue of Buddha. Vyoma set the long silver stick in front of the statue, such that the big magnifying glass faced Buddha.

"Now, let us sit in silence and meditate until the first rays of the sun enter this hall," instructed Vyoma.

Steve and Cheeka sat on either side of Vyoma and closed their eyes to meditate, while Pinkoo sat on Steve's shoulder and followed suit. For a while, there was absolute silence.

Then, an unusual sound, like the tinkling of glass, echoed in the hall. Steve opened his eyes and looked at the direction of the sound. The tinkling sound was coming from the large magnifying glass. The morning ray of the sun had touched the magnifying glass and passed through it, forming a spectrum of colors. The multicolored rays of the spectrum converged again into a dot. This beautiful dot of light touched the Buddha's forehead, just between the eyes. Gradually, the dot grew bigger, and the golden statue started glowing.

Steve looked around to find that Vyoma was still deep in meditation. Cheeka and Pinkoo, as wide-eyed as Steve, were staring at the statue.

And just then, the statue started to turn around and shift from its base. As the statue moved, it revealed a gold box under it.

Now, Vyoma opened his eyes and spoke. "Go and bring that box, Steve."

Steve picked up the box and brought it with him. Vyoma then walked up to the statue and removed the magnifying glass from its stand. As the converged spot of light moved away, the statue of Buddha turned back to its original position.

Vyoma opened the gold box and pulled out a scroll from within it. Though the scroll appeared ancient, it was intact. As Vyoma opened it, Steve noticed that it was made of a very unusual cloth. The cloth was transparent. At the center of the cloth was a map of the world.

And, it was no ordinary map. The borders of the countries in the map and all other objects appeared animated. The clouds were travelling, winds were blowing, the oceans were vibrant with waves, the sun was rising and the moon was setting. The topography of all the nations were shown to the last detail—from the mountain to the plateaus; the rivers and the lakes; the fields and the deserts; the snow-capped peaks of majestic mountains to the boiling lava in the erupting volcanoes. It was like our bountiful earth, in all its diversity, waiting to be discovered. Amazingly, one could see through that transparent, animated map.

"What kind of a map is this?" Steve asked Vyoma.

Vyoma smiled at him and said, "This is the secret scroll. It's a unique guide for anyone who knows nothing about our world. A gateway to the discovery of our planet. It holds within itself the history, wisdom and knowledge of all the ancient civilizations."

"But I can understand nothing in this map. I see no cities, no destinations," said Steve, "just mountains, fields, rivers, deserts, oceans, and volcanos. How would I know where to start, and which way to go? And what about the paintings? I don't see the seven places where they have been hidden? I don't see how this map will help me."

"Remember what Master told you. The secret of the seven destinations is hidden in the Valley of Flowers," said Vyoma. "This map is just the base to your expedition. It shows the vast and glorious field in which you will now commence your quest. Most importantly, this map is alive and deeply linked to Mother Nature. It will warn you against approaching natural calamities and other dangers in your route. It will protect you against any evil forces that might harm you. This is Buddha's gift to you. Take extreme care of it.

"Now, it's time for you to go with this scroll to the Valley of Flowers. From here on, it's your journey. You have to proceed on your own. Our blessings are always with you. May God be with you!"

"I have a request to make," said Steve. "Could I please take Cheeka and Pinkoo with me? Without them, I will be lonely."

"Well, I suppose you can. They have been your partners ever since you came here. You three can be one another's support on this expedition too. I wish the three of you all success." Saying this, Vyoma blessed them.

Carrying some clothes and food in cloth bundles, the three of them left for the Valley of Flowers.

Both Cheeka and Pinkoo knew the route. They went behind the monastery and took the narrow lane that led to a forest. The forest was dense, with tall trees and thick bushes growing all over. A light wind blew through the trees, making a soft whistling sound. Sunlight filtered through the branches creating hundred patterns along the path. Dry leaves crackled under their feet, breaking the otherwise silent ambience.

As they moved forward, the trees grew taller and denser. Their branches and leaves were so thick and interwoven that the rays of the sun could not penetrate through them. The visibility was reducing; but they moved on.

After walking a little longer, they reached what seemed to be a dead end. The path ended abruptly at a steep rock face. There was no way they could climb this high precipice.

"What do we do now?" asked Steve. "Are you sure we are on the right path?"

"I can fly over this," said Pinkoo. "The Valley of the Flowers is on the other side of this rock face. I have been there many times with the other butterflies from the Butterfly Nest."

"But how do we go there?" Steve was worried.

"Nothing is impossible, when you are with Cheeka!" said Cheeka grinning. "Come with me." Cheeka took them a few steps to their right, into the forest. Passing through the thick bushes they spotted the hollow trunk of a tree. It seemed that the tree had been cut. It had two hollow branches on either side. There were no leaves on these branches. The trunk of the felled tree must have remained there dry and hollow for several years. Steve wondered how this one tree could have been cut in this forest that seemed so untouched! Cheeka stood at the end of one of the dry branches and said, "The Valley of Flowers is not a natural valley. It was created by one of our great masters, several ages ago. The flowers have been planted especially for all the butterflies of the Nest. This place is not known to other people. If they knew, they would take away all the flowers and our butterflies would go hungry. So a secret passage was created from here to the other end of this huge rock. This hollow tree trunk has also been artificially made. Inside this hollow tree, lies the entrance through the rock."

"Now Steve, go and stand near the other branch of this trunk." Steve did as Cheeka said.

Then, Cheeka took out a small iron ball from his bag. The ball was old and rusted. It had six iron spokes of different sizes on its surface. Showing the iron ball to Steve, he said, "See, this iron ball is actually the key to a huge lock that lies within this trunk. When I roll it into this branch, the six spokes will open six levers inside the lock. Once all the levers are opened, the iron ball will roll out of the branch beside you."

"Then, the rock behind you will open. We will have to enter the tunnel that lies hidden behind this rock surface. The entrance remains completely open for just fifteen seconds. We are three of us; so we will have to really, really rush. If one of us is left this side...I hope that doesn't happen! But if it does happen, that person will have to stay back; because the lock can open only once in twenty four hours."

Steve and Pinkoo listened to their friend, as Cheeka continued with the instructions. "Remember, as this key rolls down this branch, there will be six clicks—sound of the six levers opening. After the sixth click, the iron ball will pop out at your end. Catch it and run toward the tunnel. Get ready, Steve. Here we go!"

Cheeka put the iron ball into the hollow branch. The sound of the rolling ball could be clearly heard outside. Then it stopped, and a 'click' sound was heard.

"One," counted Cheeka.

The ball rolled on and a second 'click' was heard and then the third, fourth, and fifth clicks were heard. Then, for a few seconds the ball stopped rolling.

Steve heard something rumbling behind him. He turned around to see a huge boulder shaking, as if it would fall off the rock face. Cheeka screamed to get Steve's attention back to the grave task at hand. "Don't turn, Steve. We can't afford to get distracted. Keep your eye on the branch. The key will pop out any moment!"

But by the time Steve turned back, the sixth click was already heard, and the iron ball popped out. Steve was taken by surprise, and dropped the ball. Behind him, the huge rock started opening up.

Cheeka rushed to Steve. "Where did you drop the iron ball?" he asked in panic.

Steve was groping for the ball among the dry leaves under his feet. "It must be somewhere here."

"We can't afford to lose a second." Cheeka was panicking as the rock had completely opened to reveal the tunnel within it. "In the next ten seconds the door will close!"

But Steve could not find the ball. "Forget it!" said Cheeka. "Let's rush into the tunnel."

The rock had started closing in, when the boys ran towards it with all their strength. It was more than half closed when Cheeka jumped into the now narrow opening. He somehow managed to pull Steve into the tunnel, just before the rock completely shut with a big bang.

Cheeka and Steve turned to look ahead into the tunnel. It was pitch black.

On the other side of the rock, as if out of nowhere, a vampire bat appeared. It hovered around for a while and then dived into the dry leaves, picked up the iron ball, and flew away!

*

GROPING IN THE DARK

Steve could see nothing. He could hear only his own breathing. He called out, "Are you there, Cheeka?"

"Yes Steve, I am here. We were lucky to get in at the last moment."

"And, Pinkoo?"

"I don't know."

Cheeka and Steve called out in unison. "Pinkoo!"

There was no response.

"Pinkoo! Answer me, Pinkoo." Steve was getting worried. "Stop playing pranks in the darkness. Speak up, Pinkoo!"

Only silence.

"Pinkoo is not here, Steve," said Cheeka. "I think she could not make it."

"How can that be possible? She is so tiny and fast. She has to be in here, somewhere." Then, after a pause, he added "Can't we go out and look for her?" he asked.

"There is no way that we can go back, Steve. There is no point panicking in this darkness. First, we have got to get out of this suffocating tunnel." suggested Cheeka.

"No way," said Steve. "I am not moving an inch without Pinkoo!"

"So be it. You stay as long as you want. But I am leaving this place before breathing becomes impossible." And, Cheeka started crawling toward the other end of the tunnel.

Steve was terribly frustrated. He did not want to lose Pinkoo. But he also knew that searching for her in the darkness would be futile. Being left with no choice, he followed Cheeka. The tunnel was low and the floor was rough. Crawling through it was wounding the boys. The tunnel was not straight. There were twists and turns on the way.

After struggling for quite a while, they saw some light. The end of the tunnel could now be seen. That's when the journey became easier. Within a couple of minutes, they were on the other side of the tunnel. And when Steve stood up, the view before his eyes seemed worth all the trouble they had in the tunnel.

As far as his eyes could see, there were flowers. There were beds of white roses, spreading endlessly on all sides. In between the white flowers, there were spurts of bright colored flowers - red, blue, orange, and yellow. The flower shrubs seemed to be arranged in beautiful patterns.

The sweet fragrance of these flowers drifted everywhere, in the valley. Steve had never dreamt of so many beautiful flowers in one place. Enchanted, he closed his eyes to feel and breathe in the magical fragrance, when a voice whispered into his ear,

"Where are you lost, Steve?"

Steve opened his eyes and turned to see Pinkoo sitting on his right shoulder. "You!" he shouted out, surprised and soon, a little annoyed. "Where had you disappeared? We were looking for you all over the tunnel. Why didn't you reply? I knew you were playing a prank. This is really not fair!"

"But I was not in the tunnel," said Pinkoo. "I wanted to make sure the two of you had entered. And, I ended up being left behind."

"So how did you reach here?" Steve did not know whether to believe her.

"You forget that I can fly!" said Pinkoo. "Didn't I tell you that we butterflies regularly fly over the hill to reach here?"

"Are you two done with your greetings?" interjected Cheeka, "May I suggest that we move on?"

"Okay. What's next?" asked Steve as he looked around to figure out the way ahead.

"You need to find clues that will lead you to the seven locations where the paintings are hidden," reminded Pinkoo.

"Yes, and both of you need to tell me where to look for those clues. After all, you have been here before," said Steve.

"Yes, I've been here a couple of times. Every week, one of us is sent here to check on the flowers. But, we've never been told about any hidden clues," said Cheeka.

"So, what do we do? Where do we start?" Steve wondered aloud. He turned to Pinkoo for help. "What do you say, Pinkoo? You've come here oftener, haven't you?"

"Yes, I've come here several times, with my butterfly friends, from the Nest. But we've only come to collect nectar. Never guessed that there could be hidden clues here." Pinkoo had no idea.

"These are age old secrets that were not told to us," said Cheeka. "Only our Grandmaster knew it."

"Well, then maybe we should just search everywhere," said Steve, "Without the clues our map is useless."

That reminded him of the map he was carrying with him. "The map! Maybe this will help."

He took the map out of his cloth bundle and spread it before them. The transparent map was still alive, with flowing rivers, swaying trees, gushing water falls and lashing waves. But, there was no indication as to which of those routes would lead to the paintings. The only thing that was different was a golden star that shone at the north corner of the map.

"This is where we are," said Cheeka. "This is our guiding star that will always indicate our location.

"But the map explains nothing," said Steve. "We need to start somewhere. Like I said before, we'll just have to search everywhere in the valley. Let's search for the clues among the flowers?"

"No Steve," said Pinkoo. "The flowers are reserved for the butterflies. No one but butterflies can touch them."

"So what do I do? Stand here and gaze at the beautiful flowers forever?" Steve was getting increasingly impatient. "I am going inside. Are you coming?"

Cheeka was still reluctant. "Our Grandmaster always stopped us from entering the valley. He used to say that we selfish humans have kept everything exclusively for us. But none of us ever bothers to keep anything exclusively for the birds and animals, the butterflies and insects. Let us not enter the valley. It might harm the flowers."

"I am not going in to pluck flowers, Cheeka. I just want to find my route to the paintings. And there is nothing wrong in it." Saying this, Steve moved ahead.

"No, Steve. Don't go ahead!" warned Pinkoo.

But, Steve was not in the mood for any warning, so he continued to walk toward the flowerbeds. And as soon as he set foot among the flowers, thorny creepers grew out of the rose plants and twirled themselves around his legs. If Steve moved even an inch, the thorns would prick him. As he stood there rooted, in silence and in pain, he was startled by a voice.

"Steve, my child, impatience will never help you."

Steve knew that this was Shom's voice. "The Valley of Flowers is sacred. It was made only for the butterflies of the Butterfly Nest. If we contaminate the flowers, where will the butterflies go to collect nectar? And now, don't worry. You have our dear Pinkoo with you. She will be able to help you…out of these thorns, and to the clues!"

Steve turned toward Cheeka and Pinkoo. That's when they realized that he was stuck and hurt. They rushed to the edge of the flowerbeds where he was standing.

Cheeka held Steve's hand and tried to pull him out, but could not.

Pinkoo sat on Steve's shoulder, and then, as if by magic, the thorny creepers left Steve and he easily walked out of the flowerbed.

"Thank you both." said Steve. "Sorry, I should not have lost my patience." Then, he turned to Pinkoo. "Grandmaster spoke to me and said that you could help us find the clues."

"If that's what Grandmaster says, so I shall." And Pinkoo flew over the flowers. She went from one flowerbed to another in search of some clue, but could not find any.

Steve looked at her flying about zealously and was suddenly filled with hopelessness—the valley was immense and Pinkoo was just a little butterfly. How could she possibly cover every inch of it?

But, Pinkoo was undeterred; she flew on from flower to flower. Within some minutes, she was visibly exhausted. The speed of her flight had reduced. Steve and Cheeka watched her from a distance, but could not help her.

Steve was now more concerned about her than about the clues. "Why don't you rest for a while, Pinkoo," he said.

"I can't afford to," she answered firmly. "You know that we have little time in hand, and there is so much of the valley still left to search."

"How about you fly higher a get a bird's eye view of the whole valley? Suggested Steve, "Or should I say a butterfly's eye view!"

Pinkoo laughed as she moved up a bit. It looked

like it was not easy for her. But she garnered all the strength she could and moved even higher.

Then suddenly, she stopped mid-air. "Yes! I think I found it!" her feeble voice screamed in excitement.

But the boys could not hear her clearly. "Sorry? Can't hear you, Pinkoo. Why don't you..."

Before Steve could complete his sentence, Pinkoo continued to rattle off. "Steve, this is unbelievable!"

The boys were clueless what she was trying to say. They couldn't even figure out if she was happy, or sad, or scared, or just ranting because of tiredness.

It was Cheeka's turn to get impatient this time. "Hey princess, flying up above the world so high...we mere mortals standing on mother earth have gone deaf. Could you kindly step down to talk to us?"

Pinkoo sensed the irritation in Cheeka's voice and flew back to the boys, unaware of the bat, which was flying much above her.

Pinkoo was circling Steve and Cheeka, fluttering her wings in exhilaration, as she chanted "It's amazing; it's just amazing!"

"How could I never notice this wonderful secret hidden in the valley of flowers?" Pinkoo continue. "I have come here so often, but never paid attention!"

"What is it?" asked Cheeka.

"The clues! They are all hidden in the flowerbeds," said Pinkoo.

"Well, what are they?" asked Steve.

"I can't explain it from here;" said Pinkoo, "you have to see the flowerbeds from up there to understand what I am saying."

"In that case, we just need to fly!" said Cheeka sarcastically. "All I need is a pair of wings!"

"Come on Cheeka," pacified Steve. "Don't get so irritated. Without Pinkoo's help, we would reach nowhere."

Pinkoo glided and perched herself proudly on Steve's shoulder, as he continued, "We should actually try to understand what she wants to say. Let's see...we need to a get a bird's eye view of the flowerbeds."

Steve turned around hoping to find some way. His eyes stopped at the rock face through which they had come. "Yes, we should climb to the top of the rock face," he said, as he picked up the map and started walking towards it, with Pinkoo on his shoulder. Cheeka followed, still a little agitated.

They walked about for some time, only to realize how impossible it would be to climb the rock face. It was one solid rock with no tree on it. There was nothing to hold on to.

The boys stood there looking at each other. "Where do we start?" asked Steve.

Cheeka's weariness was apparent in his unenthusiastic response. "I don't know. I don't think this is good idea. I can see no path; nothing to hold on to. And we have none of those mountaineering gadgets."

"But, if the flowers of the valley have been arranged to indicate a route, and the flower arrangement can be understood only from a height, then there has to be a way to reach the top of this great rock," said Pinkoo, whose spirits never seemed to dull. "The Grandmasters of our monastery must have created something. We are surely missing it."

"I agree. Let's think about all that we've seen of this rock face," said Steve. "How about we go back to the tunnel's exit, where we came out from?" His partners agreed.

On reaching the exit, they realized that the mouth of the tunnel was closed with a big boulder. There was no visible sign of any path leading to the top of the hill. The boys looked around for some outlet or clue, somewhere. All they could see were stones of different shapes and sizes. They picked up stones, moved big rocks in search of clues, but could not find any.

Pinkoo also tried to help them. She flew over stones, peeped into holes, but it didn't help. As she flew a little away from the spot, she noticed a small rose plant with a blooming red rose. Strangely, the plant was growing on a rock.

Pinkoo's butterfly senses were very attracted to the rose, so she went and sat on it. She was startled when the plant started to creep back into stone. Frightened, Pinkoo flew away and watched the plant from a distance. The plant along with the rose disappeared into the stone. Then, the stone started to roll. It rolled for a while until it hit a large rock next to it. The rock started to slide away creating a rumbling sound. The boys heard the rumbling sound and saw Pinkoo pointing to the rock. When they reached the moving rock, they found that there was an old brass handle hidden behind it and that was in plain view now.

"What is all this about?" asked Steve.

"I have no idea," said Pinkoo and described what had happened when she sat on the red rose.

Cheeka was familiar with such events. "If I'm not mistaken, this should be the key to another passage," he said. "But it could also be a trap. Let me pull this knob and see what happens." He pulled the handle with all his strength, but nothing happened.

"Let me give you a hand," said Steve. The boys tried with all their might but were disappointed when nothing happened.

That's when Pinkoo came up with another idea. "Why don't you try to twist and turn the handle, instead of pulling it?" she said.

The boys turned it to the left. With a creaking sound an inch of the handle came out of the rock.

"Let's turn it to the other side," said Steve. This time they turned it to the right. The earth beneath them started shaking. A large cylindrical portion of the rock face that was attached to the handle moved out of the rock face and was slowly falling to the ground. As it came out, there was a huge crack in the rock face—right from the base to the top.

Steve clutched Cheeka's hand, afraid that they were about to witness an earthquake. But, Cheeka felt otherwise. "This is our path to the top." Cheeka's positive self was back in place.

"If this crack is a path, how do we walk through it?" wondered Steve.

"There has to be something more," guessed Cheeka. "Is it possible that..."

Before Cheeka could say it, the rock cylinder,

which had come out of the rock face and was now parallel to ground, slowly started to roll through the crack and move upwards.

"This is it!" said Cheeka excitedly. "Steve, this cylinder will take us to the top of this rock. Let's hop on to it."

"But, how?" wondered Steve. "How can I stand on a rolling cylinder? This would be like trying to walk on a road roller. If we slip, we will go under the road roller and get crushed into a pulp."

"We've got to give it a try, Steve. If we miss this chance, we might never be able to climb up. Just jump on the cylinder. Once we're on it, we'll try to balance by walking against the direction of the rolling cylinder."

The earth was shaking; stones were falling off the rock face. The friction created by the huge cylindrical stone moving within the rock face was making a big noise; and there was a lot of smoke and dust. Steve was reminded of the horrifying experience he had had in the Secret chamber. He was too nervous to move.

The cylinder was picking up speed. Cheeka knew that there was no time to waste. He grabbed Steve's hand and jumped onto the cylinder. But Steve was unprepared and did not land on it. And Cheeka couldn't get a grip on Steve's hand. Moreover he had to balance himself on the cylinder.

Steve would have fallen off the cylinder, which was now at least six feet above the ground. But he somehow managed to hang on to the cylinder which was constantly rotating. Steve could not hang on for much longer.

Cheeka, who was balancing by constantly walking against the rolling cylinder, had no choice but to watch Steve fall off the cylinder. Steve would have come crashing to the ground, if he hadn't got a grip on the brass handle attached to the cylinder. However, the brass handle had become very hot because of the constant friction of the rocks. His hand started burning and he could not bear to hold on to the handle any longer. But, the cylinder had caught momentum. It was rushing up the hill. Loosening the grip now would mean falling down more than a hundred meters. Steve had no choice but to shift his grip from one hand to the other. He did not know how long his other hand could bear the pain of the burning palm, as he held on to the increasingly hot handle.

On the rotating cylinder, Cheeka was also struggling hard. As the cylinder moved faster, the rotation was faster, which meant he had to walk backward at a greater speed. The smoke produced by the friction of the stones had grown so heavy by now, that he was loosing sight of Steve. He could not see Pinkoo either and wondered where she had disappeared.

Cheeka shouted out, "Steve, can you hear me?" His voice seemed to die out with the loud noise of the moving rock cylinder.

While continuing his tightrope backward walk on the cylinder, Cheeka tried to extend his hand downward and shouted even louder than before. "Give me your hand, Steve!"

"I can't see you, Cheeka!" said Steve's voice.

"Never mind, my friend. Just extend your hand."

Somewhere in the smoke he could faintly see Steve's hand. Cheeka bent as much as he could.

As Steve tried to reach out, his other hand's grip on the handle kept loosening. Finally, Steve gave up. He could not bear the terrible heat of the brass handle. He let the handle go. Barely fifty meters from the top of the rock face, Steve let go.

"No! Steve, no!" shouted Cheeka in desperation as he failed to get a grip on his friend's hand. Suddenly, all the noise and movement stopped. The cylinder had reached the top of the mountain.

Cheeka stepped out and sat at the edge of the rock face, exhausted. The cylinder rolled back down the mountain and it went back to its original, vertical position. The rumbling sound faded out. Cheeka sat silently on the rock as tears rolled down his eyes. His mission seemed to have come to an end abruptly. He had lost his friend Steve and there was no sign of Pinkoo either. He stared blankly at the thick cloud of smoke that was still surrounding him.

As Cheeka sat in silence, he felt a gentle breeze blowing all around him. Gradually, the wind got stronger. The smoke started clearing. Cheeka was not sure what was happening, as the speed of the wind was increasing rapidly. Strangely, the wind was not coming down from the sky; it seemed to come from the earth.

Soon, the wind grew into a storm, and the smoke totally disappeared. And this time, Cheeka stared with complete amazement!

From under the mountain, appeared millions of butterflies, holding each other's hands. The storm that he was experiencing was created by the fluttering of their wings. But the real surprise was yet to come. As the great net of butterflies came up, Cheeka was dumbfounded to see Steve in the center of it. His dear friend was alive and safe. And so was Pinkoo, who was sitting proudly on Steve's nose. The wonderful butterflies brought him to the top of the mountain and placed him softly on the ground. Cheeka was overwhelmed. He rushed toward his friend and hugged him.

"Steve! Steve, you're alive! I thought I had lost you. I'd have never forgiven myself for not being able to save you." Cheeka's voice was trembling with happiness. "How did this miracle happen?"

"It's all thanks to Pinkoo! As usual, she was there at the right time!" said Steve, and turned to Pinkoo, who was proudly fluttering her wings on Steve's right shoulder.

Steve began narrating the tale of being saved by his dear friends, the butterflies of the Nest. "Remember, at one point you stretched your hand toward me? I tried my best to catch your hand. But because of the smoke, I could not see your hand clearly. And the handle I was holding had become so hot that I had to let go of it. I closed my eyes and was prepared for the big crash; but it ended as feather bounce. It was very breezy, almost windy. I though I was already dead and flying toward heaven, when I heard Pinkoo's voice. I opened my eyes to see her lovely face smiling at me. I realized that I'd landed on these million butterflies."

"Pinkoo had rushed to the Nest to get them, when she saw that I hadn't landed on the cylinder. Thanks to Pinkoo, I am alive." Overwhelmed with emotion, Pinkoo hugged Steve's nose with her wings. Steve kissed her bright pink wings affectionately.

Cheeka ran forward to hug Steve and Pinkoo. The butterflies spread out around them, filling the space with myriad colors. The Queen of the butterflies flew up to Pinkoo and placed a crown made of golden petals on her little head. All the butterflies flapped their wings, creating a fragrant breeze all over.

"We are proud of you," said the Queen. "This crown will always protect you, wherever you go. If you ever need our help, just rub your wings on this crown and help will be by your side."

She then flew up to speak to the boys. "We are aware that the three of you are on an important mission. God's blessings and our Master' grace will support you all through. We shall always be there with you. Now it's time for us to collect nectar. It's time for us to bid farewell for now."

The Queen was just about to fly away, when Pinkoo called out. "Please Queen, don't go now."

"Why?" asked the queen.

"If all of you go to collect nectar, you will block Steve's view of the valley. They've come up here to get a bird's eye view of the flowers, which have been arranged in a certain pattern," said Pinkoo, as the other butterflies looked at her in surprise.

"So be it, my child," said the Queen. She turned to

address the other butterflies. "Let us make way for our Pinkoo and her friends."

The butterflies moved and the boys walked past them to the edge of the rock face. Pinkoo pointed out to Steve and Cheeka. "Look carefully, the entire valley is filled with white roses. In between these white flowers are bunches of colored flowers. And these bunches of colored flowers are joined with green shrubs. Doesn't this look like some kind of a well planned pattern?"

"Yes, you are right," said Cheeka, as his eyes brightened. "The flowers are set in the order of the colors of the rainbow. It starts with the color violet and ends with the color red. Did you notice that Steve?"

"Yes, of course," he said. "These are the seven colors of our seven paintings. And the green shrubs joining these colors indicate some kind of a route. But if this is a route, how would we know where the route starts and which direction to follow?"

The trio fell silent. The buzzing of the butterflies also stopped, when all of a sudden Pinkoo burst out "There it is!"

"What's wrong with you?" began a startled Cheeka. "Why do you keep scaring us?"

"Why are we wasting our time when we have a map to refer to?" she replied in excitement.

"Yes, yes, how could I forget?" said Steve as he quickly took out the map and spread it on the ground. Everyone studied the map carefully. As usual, everything in the map was animated and a golden star showed their present location on the rock face, facing the Valley of Flowers. That's when the boys noticed that here was no similarity between the patterns of the flowers in the Valley and that shown in the map. Pinkoo kept flying into the valley and back to the map, several times. Finally she gave up and sat on Steve's shoulder, completely downcast.

The Queen butterfly was watching all of this and was not sure what they were trying to do. "I feel that you are trying to find out a route by looking at the map and observing the flowerbeds separately."

"So what do you suggest we should do?" asked Steve.

"I notice that the map is transparent. Why don't you look at the flower patterns through the map?" advised the Queen.

This was a good enough suggestion as any other. Steve lifted the map from the ground and went to the edge of the mountain. Steve and Cheeka lifted it in front of them. Through the transparent map, they could see the whole valley clearly.

The map started swaying around. Steve and Cheeka held on to it tightly, fearing it would fly out of their hands. But the movement of the map was stronger than their grip. They were sure it will fall of.

The Queen butterfly saw this and said, "The map is not flying away because of the breeze. You see the wind around us is soft and gentle. The map looks like it needs to free itself so that it can adjust itself to the flower pattern. Let it go!"

Steve and Cheek let go of the map. It rotated around, mid-air, and halted such that the flower patterns fitted exactly into the map. Through the transparent map the boys could see seven destinations clearly marked in seven parts of the globe. The green shrubs showed the route that joined the seven destinations. Gradually, the impression of the flower patterns got imprinted on the map and the map flew back into Steve's hand.

The butterflies started fluttering their wings again and the boys were overjoyed. The Queen flew into the sky along with all the other butterflies. They filled the sky with colors; they formed different patterns, and finally wrote 'Good Luck' on the sky. Steve, Cheeka, and Pinkoo waved at them as they stooped down to the flowers to collect nectar.

The sky was clear and the sun was shining bright. The boys took a closer look at the map. Their first destination was marked by the first color of the rainbow, 'Violet'. This destination was in Alaska. Steve had heard of Alaska and its difficult terrain. Now the question was, "How to reach there?" They had no means of transport and no idea about the route.

"Well, at least we have the map and know about the seven destinations," said Steve.

Cheeka was silent for a while. He finally spoke. "But, we don't know where to start."

Now both the boys went silent. Pinkoo watched the sadness that was creeping into their faces.

"Why are you so sad?" she asked.

"You know how difficult things appear. The map shows thousands of miles of difficult journey before us...but no clue of how to start, or where to go? What do we do?" Cheeka said.

"Will this sadness help you?" asked Pinkoo calmly.

The boys had no answer to that.

"You know this mission has been given to us by our Master. There has to be a way to solve every problem on this mission," asserted Pinkoo.

"I understand what you are saying, Pinkoo," said Steve. "If only Master was around to tell us what to! Everything appears so difficult without his presence and guidance."

"But hasn't Master guided you whenever you needed help?" asked Pinkoo. "That's true. He talks to me whenever I am in trouble" said Steve. "So why don't you trust and ask him for help?" suggested Pinkoo. Steve nodded at her, sat down calmly and closed his eyes. Cheeka and Pinkoo followed him. Steve tried to think of Shom in his mind and in his heart. As he sat in deep meditation, Steve did not realize that a dozen pairs of eyes were watching him and his friends. Up in the sky were lurking Kapaal's bats, spying on everything that the trio did. Unaware of them, Steve held the medallion gifted by Shom and communed with him. "We are at the first step of our mission and are stuck. How do we proceed with the long journey that lies ahead of us?" All the three friends desperately wanted an answer.

The touch of the medallion and the thought of his Master calmed him down. And from the depth of his heart he heard Shom's voice. "My child, you took the first step toward this mission when you left the Gompa, with everyone's blessings. And all three of you have already made good progress. As far as the rest of the journey is concerned the map will guide you. It will take you where you need to go. And why do you forget that God has given you the power of the rainbow in your own hand? Remember how you took the rays of the sun on you palm to bring the paintings to life? Be aware of your powers. The rays of the supreme power—the sun—will help you. The rest of the journey will automatically unfold before you."

"And most importantly, have faith in yourself, my boy." Shom continued. "Believe that you have achieved your goal and success will be yours. May God be with you, always!"

There was a long silence. Steve knew that his Master's voice had shown him the way. He opened his eyes and found the map floating in the air, in front of him. The sun was shining bright. Cheeka was sitting calmly and Pinkoo as usual, was on his right shoulder.

"Cheeka, Pinkoo, let's prepare to go. Hold my hand." Steve raised his right palm toward the sun. As the sunrays touched his palm, the rainbow in his palm got energized. His palm started glowing and the violet from the rainbow came out of his palm and touched the violet spot on the map. The violet ray bounced back from the map and covered the boys. The ray grew more intense. The boys were mesmerized by the violet light. A huge storm broke out; starting from the violet spot on the map, and the boys started floating over the map, mid-air. They held each other tightly. The storm grew and began to pull them toward the violet spot. And before they could realize what was happening, they were sucked into the map.

All the trio could see was violet. Violet was everywhere. They were drenched in it. Then they started travelling in mid air. In a hollow violet space, they were moving at an unimaginable speed. Steve had read about the speed of light. He felt that he was experiencing it right now. It felt like travelling through space. This was a feeling that he could only describe as "Absolutely Unreal".

Then, as the violet color started fading; everything around had changed. They were no longer at the top of a rock face. The Valley of Flowers had disappeared.

*

BELOW FREEZING POINT

Steve and Cheeka were standing in knee-deep snow. The boys turned around in amazement. "Where are we?" asked Cheeka.

"Alaska, I suppose," replied Steve. "And Pinkoo? Where is she?" He looked around and all he could see was endless landscape of snow! There was no sign of Pinkoo anywhere.

"Pinkoo!" called out Steve. He was so concerned about that delicate butterfly that he did not even realize that he was not clothed enough for the freezing cold.

He looked around and called out again. "Pinkoo! Pinkoo, can you hear me?"

"Yes…brrr...I can hear…y-y-you!" came a faint and trembling voice.

"That's Pinkoo's voice, isn't it?" he asked Cheeka, who was shivering with the cold.

"I-I..th-th-hink so…" said Cheeka.

"But I can't see her." Steve turned all around screaming, "Where are you? Pinkoo?" he asked.

"H-h-here," came the answer.

The voice seemed to come from close by. Steve looked at his right shoulder where Pinkoo used to sit. But she was not there. He looked around carefully, but could not find her. "Here? Where, Pinkoo?" he asked.

"In your p-p-pocket!" came the feeble answer.

"You are up to pranks again?" said Steve "This is not time for all this. I was so worried about you."

"W-w-what are you talking about?" said Pinkoo, shivering with cold. "It's freezing outside. I would have turned into a f-fo-fossil by now, if I had not taken shelter in your p-p-pocket. And you think I am j-jo-joking!" said Pinkoo angrily.

"I'm sorry, dear. I was so worried! I panicked, but didn't realize that you were feeling cold. I shall be careful next time." Steve then covered his pocket with his palm to give Pinkoo some warmth. That's when he realized how cold it was. They had to take shelter somewhere, as soon as possible.

"Do you have any idea about this place? Where should we go?" Cheeka asked Steve.

Steve took out the map. It unfolded and started floating mid-air. "According to this map, we're somewhere deep inside Alaska," said Steve. "I have never come here before. But I had once read about the mountains in this region. I know that we're at a very high altitude, and the oxygen level is low. I've heard that people can faint in these parts, due to lack of oxygen. And it will get much colder, once the sun sets."

The mention of 'sun' reminded Steve that he could take in the sunrays to energize himself. He raised his right palm toward the sun and held Cheeka with his left hand. Soon the rainbow on his palm started to glow and his body became warm. The growing heat in his body was passing through his left palm into Cheeka's body. This was a unique experience for Cheeka as also for Pinkoo, who was feeling comfortable and snug inside Steve's pocket. "Umm! That feels much better," she said, peeping out of Steve's pocket. "Well done, Steve! Keep it up!"

"Thank you, dear princess!" smiled Steve and looked around for a direction to proceed. As far as his eyes could see, there was snow. No houses, no humans, not even animals. He turned toward Cheeka. "What do you say, Cheeka? Which direction should we take?"

By now Cheeka was more relaxed. The warmth that he received through Steve made him feel better. He looked at the sun, which was now their only point of reference. "Why don't we start walking in the direction of the sun?"

Steve and Pinkoo agreed.

The trio started to wade through the knee-deep snow. There was a strange stillness in the air. It was probably because there were no sounds of birds or animals. Only an occasional howl of the wind would shriek through the silence. The atmosphere was such that even the kids did not talk much among themselves. An unknown land, and unknown destination; they had no choice but to keep going.

After walking for a distance, they reached some sort of a boundary that was made of blocks of ice. The transparent blocks formed a large circle, in the middle of that nowhere land.

"Stop!" said Cheeka. Pinkoo peeped out of Steve's pocket and looked around.

"What is it?" asked Steve.

"See this circle of ice?" said Cheeka solemnly.

"It looks like a big boundary made of blocks of ice," said Steve. "I am not sure if it is the boundary of a circle."

"Yes it is," assured Cheeka. "It's a rare sight, but I know about it. I have heard about it from my masters and seen ancient paintings. One gets to see such a sight in the mountain regions only once in a lifetime. It is a sacred circle of meditation. For ages some powerful soul has been meditating here." Cheeka asserted solemnly. He had grown up in the mountains and had a fair idea of the supernatural phenomenon of that region."

"Here....Where?" asked Steve.

"Inside the circle of meditation," said Cheeka.

"But I can't see a soul" said Steve.

"Wait, let me fly and find out," said Pinkoo enthusiastically.

"No...Please!" said Steve. "That's the last thing you should do, in this freezing cold. Now, let's move on."

"Wait!" said Cheeka. "I don't think we should cross the sacred circle."

"Then, what do we do?" asked Steve impatiently.

"Go around it," said Cheeka.

"It will take us hours to go around this huge circle. And if it gets dark, we will freeze to death."

"But crossing the sacred circle is not free from danger," said Cheeka, visibly scared.

"We are taking a risk, either way. Let's keep going." And Steve moved on. After a moment's hesitation, Cheeka followed him.

The sun was approaching the horizon. The kids realized that though the sun rays had kept their bodies warm, breathing was becoming very difficult. The low level of oxygen was making them feel drowsy. And, as if this was not enough, the air was suddenly filled with a strong pungent odor.

"What is that smell?" asked Steve. There was no reply. "Hey, Cheeka?" Steve asked again.

After a moment's silence Cheeka spoke slowly. "If what I am guessing is right," he said, "we better be careful!"

"But...why?" Steve asked, feeling very uncomfortable. "Where is this stink coming from?"

"Quite close to us, I feel," replied Cheeka.

"And what is it?" asked Steve, impatiently.

Before Cheeka could reply, Steve tripped on something and fell. He got up to look for the object on which he had tripped. There was something orange sticking out of the snow. Curious, Steve dug out the snow around it. Soon, he could see a florescent orange hornlike object sticking out of a hairy surface. The horn was transparent and hollow, and glowed from within. Steve tried to pull it out of the snow, but it was firmly stuck to the hairy surface.

Steve started digging around the object. It revealed a large surface covered with golden hair. Then, out came another glowing horn. It seemed like the head of a creature bigger than an elephant. What kind of a creature could it be? Steve could not recollect having read or heard of an animal with golden hair and glowing horns. Was it a prehistoric animal that humanity was not even aware of? For how many centuries had it been buried in the snow? And how come, after all these ages, the hair on its body, and the horns looked so fresh? Was the whole body of the creature intact? And the big question: was it dead or alive? Steve kept digging hard, out of curiosity.

At first Cheeka was as inquisitive and was watching the horns and hairy surface being uncovered. But by now, he had a very bad feeling about this and shouted out firmly. "Stop digging, Steve."

But Steve's curiosity was too aroused. "It looks like a unique creature that the world is not aware of. It could be a great discovery! We must share it with the world."

"That's not what we are here for," reminded Cheeka. "And this is not just any other creature."

"Well, if you know what it is, why don't you solve the riddle?" asked Steve.

Before Cheeka could reply, out sprang a large hairy ear from under the snow. It hit Steve. The impact of just the ear was so hard that Steve was thrown off several meters. Cheeka ran to rescue him, but suddenly another huge ear popped out of the snow. Cheeka tripped over it and came down with a thud. The boys were shocked out of their wits.

And now, the earth started trembling. From under the thick snow burst out columns of hot smoke. The smoke had a weird orange color and was so hot that it started melting the freezing snow around it. The tremors grew strong and wild. Steve and Cheeka narrowly escaped being hit by the shooting hot smoke. They were finding it difficult to balance themselves on the shaking earth.

"Oh God!" said Steve. "Is it an earthquake?"

"No…its..its…!" Cheeka seemed to have lost his voice.

The earth was shaking violently and the horns of the creature were glowing like fire. It appeared that some intense activity was taking place under the earth. Steve held strongly to Cheeka's hand.

"W...what's all this Cheeka?" he asked in a trembling voice. "It..It…It's the Yeti King!" shouted Cheeka struck by panic. "Run, Steve…Run for your life."

By now Steve was equally aware of the danger. With one hand on his pocket to protect Pinkoo, he ran with all his might. Cheeka followed, shouting, "We should somehow run toward the boundary of ice slabs, at the other end." But running in knee deep snow was no small task. The boys kept struggling as the tremors grew stronger, making it even more difficult for them. Suddenly everything came to a standstill with a thunder that seemed to shake all of Alaska. The boys were thrown apart. Steve looked back aghast. From under the thick layers of snow, burst out a giant animal, the size of two elephants standing on top of each other. It was like a tremendously huge man, whose body was covered with a thick coat of golden fur that glistened in the evening sun. And with two florescent horns glowing atop his head. From under his bushy eyebrows, two eyes glittered like rubies. His long heavy hands reached down, all the way to his knees. His body seemed to emanate immense heat, which caused pungent smoke all around him. Steve froze with fear. Cheeka grabbed his hand and dragged him along. "Run…For God's sake…Run, Steve," shouted Cheeka, as he pulled hard at his hand.

That's when Steve came back to his senses. He started to run behind Cheeka, with all his might. And, as expected, the mighty Yeti chased them. He had been disturbed from centuries of meditation and would severely punish the person who had troubled him. The boys were no match to the Yeti's speed and strength; but they still ran in the hope that their lives would be spared.

They knew they had to somehow cross the ice boundary. But one step of the Yeti was more than ten leaps that they could manage. Steve and Cheeka kept running with all their strength and were just about to reach the boundary, while Yeti King was just two steps behind them. He positioned himself to take a huge jump, and he would have landed on their heads, crushing them down.

The boys gathered all their strength and prepared for a final jump. But, instead of landing outside the boundary, they fell on one of the ice blocks on the boundary. The block started sinking into the snow with their weight. And before the boys could work out what was happening, they found themselves rolling down a strange tunnel. It seemed like the block was covering this tunnel and it caved in when the boys fell on it.

The walls of the tunnel were made of ice. The surface was slippery and absolutely freezing. As they went deeper into the tunnel, it got worse. The ice on the surface was biting into their skin. Breathing was getting more and more difficult. The ice tunnel took them through weird twists and turns and tumbles until they landed on a giant web made of elastic like strings of snow. The elasticity of the snow strings took the great impact with which the boys fell. Steve thanked God that they were safe, because if they had hit against a hard surface at that speed, they would have turned into pulp.

For a couple of seconds, they bounced because of the elasticity on the snowy web. Then suddenly, the web of strings threw them up with a big push. The boys went flying and fell deep into the heart of a huge cave. As they were falling, they saw long icicles hanging from the ceiling of the cave, like ropes. They tried to grip the ropes. But, when they got a hold on some ropes, the snow melted in their hands.

Steve knew that they would soon hit against the hard ice on the ground and that would be the end. And they did hit the ground. The boys closed their eyes tightly, imagining that their eyes would never open again. But they soon realized that it felt like they had landed on rose petals.

Steve took some time to open his eyes, because he thought that he might be still falling. But, when he opened his eyes, yet another incredible sight awaited him. What corner of earth was this?

*

A HIDDEN WORLD OF SNOW

The surface on which he had landed was made of small white globules of snow. The globules resembled homeopathy medicine pills. These globules were spread all over the floor and the walls of that huge cave. They also hung from the ceiling of the cave.

Steve had still not recovered from the shock of the fall. As he lay buried under thick layers of the tiny snow balls, he was amazed to realize that the snowballs covering his body kept him warm. He should have been frozen by now, but it was quite the opposite. He also realized that the snow globules were not still. Everything around him was in motion. It was as if he were floating on the surface of a calm sea. The globules would build up into a wave and pass over his body, almost drowning him. Then, they would recede, leaving him floating atop. There was constant movement on the walls and the ceiling as well.

The tiny snow balls on the wall were merging into one another forming weird figures that appeared to be alive. These abstract figures would come close to each other and then move away, forming cracks on the snowy wall. Through these cracks, a mystical violet light would fill the cave. Then, the globules would fill the crack, blocking the light. At the same time, thin but brilliant violet rays would stream into the cave through the tiny gaps between the snow globules.

Steve was lost in this play of mystical violet light and the wondrous figures on the ceiling.

There were snow globules that were hanging like stalactites from the ceiling of the cave. Steve watched them sway like the tentacles of an octopus. These swaying snow tentacles looked porous, and their pores exuded smoke that filled the cave with a misty aura.

Steve was so engrossed in this world of snow globules that he had forgotten about Cheeka and Pinkoo. Their thought suddenly filled him with fear and insecurity. He quickly reached for his pocket where he had hidden Pinkoo. But to his despair, the pocket was empty. Shocked and scared, Steve called out, "Cheeka...Pinkoo!"

His voice echoed from all corners of the cave. But there was no answer. Steve felt uneasy, with the mysterious globules crawling all over his body. He wanted to get up quickly and look around for his friends. But he was not getting a footing on the unstable floor.

After some struggle, Steve managed to stand up. But he was knee-deep in the globules. He called out for Cheeka and Pinkoo again, but got no response. He wanted to search every corner of the cave for his friends, but walking on the snow balls was almost impossible. He was not going to give up looking for the friends who had helped him through all his turmoil.

Amidst the play of violet light and shadows, he looked very carefully; searching for some glimpse of his friends. As he moved forward, he felt that he saw something moving, at the center of the cave. Cautiously, he walked in that direction. As he drew nearer, he realized that it was the hand of a kid sinking under the snow globules. Was it Cheeka? He wondered. Suddenly the sinking hand moved and Steve heard a faint voice. "Help…Please! (choke) Somebody…help!"

"Oh my God," thought Steve, shaken by the voice he had just heard. "It's Cheeka!" Steve called out with all his might, "Cheeka! Isn't that you, Cheeka?"

"Yes Steve, it's me!" Cheeka's feeble voice from under the snow continued, "Please (choke) save me Steve. But listen, don't…."

Before Cheeka could complete his sentence, Steve leapt toward him and soon realized his blunder. He felt his feet sinking, as if in a quick sand. The snow globules under his feet started turning into a whirlpool. Gradually the whole floor moved and churned like a giant whirlpool, sucking Steve into it.

But, he was more concerned about his friend, who was just a couple of feet away from him. Steve somehow wanted to grab Cheeka's sinking palm; Steve didn't realize that he was himself chest deep inside the icy quicksand. He stretched himself out with all his strength. But the more he struggled, the more he got sucked into the speeding whirlpool. At this point, all he knew was that Cheeka should be saved. And it was the love and concern for his friend that gave him the strength to take one final leap and grab Cheeka's palm. The touch of his friend gave him such a relief that he forgot that he would himself sink any moment. And that's exactly what happened. He held Cheeka's hand tightly in his hand, while he was quickly getting buried into the quicksand.

Steve was submerged all the way to his neck, and the level of the snow globules continued to rise. Within moments, Steve was gasping for breath. His body seemed to be entering an infinite hole. Although he still held on to Cheeka's hand, Steve finally felt that the end had come. All his efforts, his entire struggle was going to be futile. With his eyes barely above the quicksand, a breathless Steve felt his vision dwindling. With his blurred vision, he thought he saw a spot of pink fluttering The pink spot came close to him very quickly and he heard a voice that lifted up his fading spirits. "Steve!" shouted the familiar voice.

"I can't believe this! Pinkoo?" he shouted back, while trying to get a better look through the globules that filled his eyes. As he opened his mouth to talk, the globules gushed into his throat and he began choked.

"Don't talk, Steve," said Pinkoo, "hold on to this quickly."

Steve saw that with her tiny legs Pinkoo was tightly holding a long tentacle hanging from the ceiling. She flew with all her strength with the tentacle, toward Steve. In fact, the tentacle was stretching like an elastic band as she pulled it toward Steve with all her tiny strength. But with every inch of progress that Pinkoo made, she found Steve going further away from her, as he sank into the globules. His head was already below the snow. He held his breath because he knew that if he tried to breathe the globules would get into his mouth and nose, and choke him. He could not open his eyes as they were burning because of the globules scraping against them. He was loosing his senses fast. There was just enough energy left in him to hold on to Cheeka's hand and keep another hand out of the quicksand. Everything seemed to be in vain, as Steve felt his spirit sinking.

Just inches above him little Pinkoo was using her last bit of strength to hold on to the stretched tentacle hanging from the ceiling. There was tremendous elasticity in the tentacle and it created a great backward thrust. But, for Pinkoo this was the last hope to save her friends. Her tiny legs were trembling, but she knew that if she left the tentacle, it would spring back to the roof and that would be the end of her friends. She prayed to God and asked her grandmaster Shom for help. "Oh master, please come to our help," she prayed silently.

Inside the mirror maze, Shom was frozen in the mirror trap where he had kept the evil Kapaal captive. Shom knew that as long as he was there, the powerful black magician could not move an inch. But he also knew that his disciples were in trouble.

Pinkoo's desperate thought waves reached him and the center of his forehead started to glow, like a third eye. Shom focused his thought waves on the kids, as a beam of violet light came out of his forehead and traveled with tremendous speed, until it penetrated the cave filled with snow globules.

In the cave, violet waves merged with the violet light of the cave. The resulting violet beam forged to the center of the whirlpool and touched Steve's forehead.

A new lease of life surged through Steve's body, as the violet light filled him. As he was coming around, he heard his Master's voice. "Steve, my child, trust in the presence of God inside you. Don't forget the power of the Rainbow on your palm. Just focus on your strength and God will help you".

Steve felt as if he had woken up from a deep slumber. His body was completely submerged in the snow globules. But he was fully aware that he was holding Cheeka with his left hand and his right palm was sticking out of the quicksand.

The palm was the only trace of Steve that Pinkoo could see and this was her last hope. She knew that she could not hold on to the string anymore. She had exhausted all her energy and her tiny wings could not flutter. The elasticity of the tentacle had now started pulling her backward. She was just an inch away from Steve's palm, when she felt herself being pulled back. She knew that the moment she left the tentacle, it would spring back. Filled with hopelessness, she was in tears and was about to give up. That's when Steve's palm started glowing; and out came the brightest rainbow that pulled the tentacle toward him.

Blinded by the unexpected bright rainbow, Pinkoo lost her grip on the tentacle and fell down. She had used the last bit of her strength and could fly no more. She was free-falling, and realized that the tentacle must have bounced back to the roof. Suddenly, she saw a vivid image of Steve and Cheeka drowning into the globules. She opened her eyes with a jolt, and screamed, "No! This can't be!" And she saw before her the answer to her prayers.

Powerful rainbow rays emanating from Steve's palm were acting like a powerful magnet and the tentacle was following its command. It submissively moved toward him, until he had a good grip of it. And as soon as Steve clutched it, the huge whirlpool came to a stand still. The tentacle vibrated as its elasticity was giving way to the strong influence of Steve's delicate palm.

Steve knew that if he pulled the tentacle further, it would snip and all efforts would be in vain. So, he lightly tugged at the tentacle and leapt out of the globule swamp, while holding on to Cheeka.

The tentacle that was stretched beyond its limit pulled the two kids out like lightning and up they went flying toward the ceiling of the cave.

Before they could touch the ceiling, the entire cave was filled with a bright violet luminescence. The snow tentacle carrying the boys started gravitating toward the source of that light—a huge opening in the wall.

The boys reached the other side of the wall

through the opening, and they were transported into a world that was beyond anything that the mind can comprehend.

They were at least thirty feet above the ground, when Steve lost his grip on the tentacle. Even Cheeka slipped from his hand. A freefall from that height would have been fatal. All Steve could do was pray that they survive this fall by some miracle.

And a miracle did happen. Although they had been thrown up at a great speed, their fall downwards was slow and gentle. In fact, Steve felt like he was floating. It felt as if they were on the moon, where the gravitational pull is not too strong.

Steve touched the ground like a feather. The place where he landed was bathed in violet rays. As Steve looked around, he realized that he was actually standing inside a huge crystal ball. Strangely, the walls of the crystal ball, which should have been reflecting the violet rays, seemed blurred. He then realized that the walls of the crystal sphere were actually rotating at a great speed. It was probably because of this high-speed rotation that the gravitational pull of this place was reduced.

As soon as he thought of the reduced gravitation, he wanted to test it again. So, he jumped up with all his might and went as high as ten feet up. He was amazed and was enjoying the near floating experience, when something else caught his attention.

From that height, he could see that the violet rays pervading this huge crystal ball were emerging from a bright spot on one end. Steve could get a glimpse of this source of light and felt something unusual about it.

When he landed on the ground, he stood for a while, pondering. What was unusual about the violet light source?

Something struck Steve and he sprang up for another jump. This time he focused on the light source, although the rays were blinding. Steve had to strain his eyes to get a better view of what he thought he had glimpsed earlier. After a while, when his eyes got used to the brilliance, he saw that the source looked like a cobweb of violet rays. A cobweb that was animated and alive! And in the middle of the cobweb was fluttering a colored creature. It was Pinkoo!

"No!" shouted Steve, as he landed on the ground. He soon realized that Cheeka was missing too. "Why do I have to be separated from my friends like this every time?"

Steve tried to listen attentively to any sound, any hint of where Cheeka was. Then he heard it—a very faint and weak "Mmm...mmm..."

"Cheeka, my friend!" he shouted. "If you can hear me, please reply."

"Mmmm....!" The same sound for a reply!

It was Cheeka's voice, Steve was sure. He rushed toward the voice. But he reached a partition made of snow globules. The globules were same kind that he had seen on the other side of the cave, before he ended up inside this crystal ball. Where could Cheeka be? Steve distinctly heard the voice behind him.

"Mmmm...," that voice again. This time Steve was sure that the voice was coming from behind the wall of snow globules.

Steve struck the snow globule partition with his shoulder. The globules went flying in the air and Steve fell on the other side of the wall. And yes, Cheeka was in front of him. Only, he was not too happy to see him like that. Cheeka was lying down. Hundreds of thin white strings ran all over his body, tying him down. These strings were nailed to the floor with white globules. Steve rushed to Cheeka and held out his hand. "How did this happen to you, my friend? Who tied you up like this?"

Cheeka could not utter a word; his mouth was sealed with the white strings. There were strings tied across every inch of his body. From his head to his toe, he was all tied up. Every hair on his head was nailed to the floor. His ears were tied. His nose was pressed so hard by the queer thin white strings that he could hardly breathe. Even his eyebrows were nailed to the floor with those strings. He could barely open his eyes. In deep agony he looked at Steve, as if he was trying to say something. Steve could not bear to see his friend in such pain. Steve wondered how Cheeka got into this terrible situation. They had been apart for only a few minutes. Who tied him up? There was not a soul around.

Steve realized that there was no point in wasting time over these questions. He had to rescue his friend, without further delay. The strings were very thin and Steve thought that he could break them easily. But they were so many, and they were tied so tightly that Steve could not decide where to begin.

He managed to grip a bunch of strings tied to

Cheeka's chest. He was about to pull it when Cheeka mumbled something. Steve looked at him. Cheeka was trying hard to say something; but his mouth was all tied up. All Steve could understand from his expression was pain, and maybe some kind of warning. But what was Cheeka trying to warn him about? Steve had no time to think. He only knew that he had to free Cheeka from this mysterious captivity and then, Pinkoo from that weird violet web. There was no time to lose. Hurriedly Steve pulled hard at the thin white strings hoping that they would snip instantly. But the strings turned out to be much stronger than he had imagined. He pulled again, harder this time. But things got worse. The harder he pulled, the harder the strings tightened on Cheeka's body.

"Mmmm....!" Cheeka let out a painful groan. Now Steve realized what Cheeka was trying to say earlier. If he pulled at the strings any harder, it would dig into Cheeka's skin.

Steve let go of the strings and wondered what he should do next. He did not want to leave his friend in this condition. On the other hand there was Pinkoo caught in the mysterious web. As he stood there, totally lost, he did not realize that there was a mysterious activity on the floor that he stood. He suddenly heard Cheeka's painful voice behind him. He turned back swiftly, to see that weird sight...

Thousands of ice globules from the floor of the cave were fast advancing toward him. Although they looked like sweet little globules, they looked formidable right then. It seemed that they would attack Steve, who stood wondering what his next move should be.

Once again he heard Cheeka's muffled shriek. He looked at Cheeka whose eyes wore a panicked expression. He was frantically trying to say something to Steve.

Soon, Steve felt the globules climbing up his legs. He stamped his feet trying to free himself; but they stuck on. The globules had already reached his ankle. His only option was to run away from the spot. So, with all his strength he ran toward the source of light, hoping to reach the violet web and free Pinkoo. But due to the weak gravitational pull, his feet could not move forward at a good speed. The globules were fast catching up with him. Finally, he decided that there was no point in struggling to free his feet from the tiny snow balls. He would rather crush them with his hands. So he bent down, took a handful of the globules and smashed them into a lump. He worked hard and fast and soon his legs were free.

He hurried again to reach Pinkoo. But his running was like a slow motion shot in a movie. He wished that he could run much faster. If only the power of gravity was normal! He had taken a few strides when a strange sound behind him made him look back. He saw that the globules that he had crushed into lumps were changing their shapes. They were turning into tiny human figures that looked like soldiers. Little soldiers made of ice! These miniature warriors seemed to belong to another period and were fully equipped with armors, helmets, and weapons. In awe, Steve watched as the ice warriors were fast multiplying. More globules were coming together and forming many more of those tiny creatures. And they were all alive and marched toward him in unison.

One of the warriors who looked stronger than the others came forward and took the lead. He took out his spear and held it high above his shoulder. In a faint voice, which must have been loud enough for his size, he let out a sound. Steve could hear his voice but did not understand his alien language. But he knew that the leader's voice was communicating an order. And immediately, the entire battalion, which numbered in hundreds now, followed the leader and raised their spheres. Steve was amused by the incredible behavior of the cute-looking little creatures. He wanted to play with them. He bent down wanting to pick up their leader.

His amusement soon turned into shock when he heard the leader blurting out a mighty war cry. Steve saw the leader throwing a spear at him. It would have struck his nose, if Steve had not jumped back. Thanks to Steve's quick action, the spear fell near his toe. A thin white string was attached to the sphere. The string wrapped itself around Steve's foot. Steve pulled up his feet thinking that the thin string would easily break. But he was wrong. Nothing happened to the string. Before he could think of another move, all the soldiers followed their leader and threw spears at Steve. In a flash, hundreds of spears flew in the air and struck near his legs. Tiny strings attached to all those spears tied themselves around his legs. Steve fell down on his face, with a thud.

He was not going to give in easily. He had to save his friends. He pulled at his legs with all his strength. But the harder he pulled, the deeper the strings dug into his skin. Now he knew what had happened to poor Cheeka. Lying on his chest he was thinking hard about all the possible ways of getting out of the situation. His legs were tied, but his hands were still free. "If only I could break or cut the strings!" he thought.

Suddenly, he remembered that he had been given a small knife by the inmates of the Gompa, before he left for the expedition. He quickly searched for it and found it in his back pocket. The moment he tried to cut the thin strings, the blade of the knife became cold. Steve realized that the strings were made of snow. The knife was soon covered with ice. The knife froze and Steve had to let go of it.

The warriors, while moving closer to Steve, picked up globules, which magically turned into spears. Within moments, more spears were hurled at Steve. Every part of his body was tied and pinned to the ground. Steve somehow managed to keep his head above the ground, so he could see ahead of him. He felt so handicapped and dejected, lying on the floor and not being able to move. He was reminded of the story 'Gulliver's travel,' that he had heard at the orphanage. He felt like Gulliver, who was also held captive by tiny people.

But these were no little people, these were strange creatures made of ice. Steve saw the creatures morph back into ice globules as they scattered away. With them, the violet light around him started moving away. The fast spinning walls of the crystal sphere slowed down and came to a halt. With this the gravitational pull increased and Steve's body felt heavier. He felt exhausted, weak, and very lonely.

*

HOPING AGAINST HOPE.

Steve started revisiting the chain of events that had stormed through his life within a period of barely a week, since he was sent off from his home in New York.

He was filled with thoughts of his friends back in the Holy Family orphanage…his home, which was now thousands of miles away. Though life was tough there and he had faced many hardships, the orphanage was the place where he had grown up. He was reminded of the bakery where he used to bake cakes, pastries and buns. It was just about a week back when he was baking dry fruits buns for Christmas. "Oh my God!" he thought, "Christmas should be just around the corner. And this will be the first time in all these years that I will not be with my friends to celebrate Christmas."

Steve had lost track of the days and did not know when Christmas would arrive. "Who knows, whether people in this part of the world have even heard of Christmas?" he thought, as his heart sank.

Lying flat on his face he felt helpless and

insecure. He prayed to God and called out to Shom for help. And as if God had heard his prayers, the walls of the cave started rotating again. As their speed grew, his body felt lighter and he could breathe more easily. Gradually, the violet rays grew brighter and Steve felt that the source, from which the rays were emerging, was coming toward him. He looked carefully and felt that the violet web was growing bigger. It was obviously advancing toward him. He hoped that it will not bring him further trouble.

His fear transformed into hope when he saw a faint vision of colored wings fluttering. Could it be?

Yes, it was Pinkoo! Steve heaved a sigh of relief, thanking God she was alive. But he decided to lie low so that no more trouble comes to Pinkoo.

Pinkoo was still caught in the web of rays. However, she did not appear to be hurt, even though she was captive in the web. Steve was finding it difficult to look at the brilliant light around Pinkoo, but he did not want to keep his eyes off her. As Pinkoo with the violet aura came closer to him, Steve felt that the source of the light was not something abstract as it had appeared from a distance. It was actually the figure of a creature. And what an unusual creature it was! The creature was just about a foot tall, with a body that appeared to be made of snow. Fluffy snow that had a shape, but the shape was not definite. It was like a piece of cloud that had taken a human sort of form. This snow white figure had a head that was larger than the rest of his body. He wore a long and flowing beard that reached up to his knees. The face was chubby and had a cute button-like nose.

The only thing on his body that had color was a pair of gleaming blue eyes that shone brightly from under flowing white eye brows. In sharp contrast to his soft snowy body was the armor that he wore. This glistening armor was made of hard, sharp edged ice. The strong armor gave him a robust look and the shining ice helmet resting on two big round ears made him look truly like the leader of the battalion of ice soldiers.

As the leader walked toward him, Steve noticed two more peculiar features. One, he was not walking, but floating a few inches above the ground. Second, the bright violet rays were actually emitting from the center of his forehead. These violet rays had woven a web in which Pinkoo was captive. The figure came close to Steve and his blue eyes looked deep into his. Steve felt a series of ice cold waves travel through his body.

In the midst of all these distractions, Steve's attention was fixed on his friend. "Are you okay, Pinkoo?" asked Steve softly.

Pinkoo looked straight at him, but could not talk.

"Say something, little one," said Steve.

Pinkoo just kept looking back at him, without uttering a word. She appeared to be under a hypnotic spell.

"She can't talk," informed a deep, rumbling voice. Steve looked around to see who was talking. There was no one but the small creature in front of him. But he couldn't have spoken, because his lips did not move.

"Who are you?" asked Steve looking around and

why are you hiding?"

"I am not hiding anywhere; I am right in front of you." This time Steve was sure the voice came from the creature facing him, although the lips still did not move.

"Did you talk to me?" he asked.

"Yes, of course!" said the creature.

"How can I hear you, when you haven't even opened your mouth?" asked Steve, bewildered and irritated.

"That's because I communicate with you through my thoughts" said the creature.

"What a weird creature?" thought Steve. "He must be an alien, from some other galaxy."

"No, I am not an alien," said the creature. "We all belong to Earth."

"Are you...are you reading my thoughts?" asked Steve.

"Yes. I can read your thought as simply as I communicate with you through my thoughts" he said.

Steve was reminded of his grandmaster Shom who could also communicate to him with his thoughts. But he wondered how another creature could have such an incredible power which he thought only his master possessed.

"If you are not an alien, how come you are so different? You do not seem to belong to any species present on earth."

"We belong to the human race." said the creature. "But we are far more advanced than you. Our bodies do not perish like yours. We belong to this sacred ice land and live a life which is frozen in time. There is no beginning or end to our lives. We keep changing our form, depending on the situation."

"So, your present situation demanded that you recruit your entire battalion to capture two unarmed boys and a tiny butterfly?" said Steve, who was quite cheesed off by now.

"This is not a battalion," said the creature. "We are the Viola Tribe. For centuries we have been deputed to protect the earth from evil forces. You three are intruders into our world. This is why you have been held captive."

"We did not mean to intrude," said Steve. "We had no clue about this secret world. It was an accident that brought us here." Steve went on to describe how they accidentally tripped on the Yeti and in a frantic attempt they bumped onto the ice slab and slid into the tunnel.

The leader of the Violas listened to him attentively. After thinking for a while, he talked again without moving his lips. "One thing is clear...you are not lying." Steve watched the creature silently as he went on. "But, I wonder how you are still alive!"

Steve could clearly see the change in the leader's expression as his blue eyes shone brightly, looking directly into his own eyes. "Not many humans have seen the Yeti," he continued; "And those who have seen him are not alive. The one you saw is, in fact, the king of the Yetis...the supreme, powerful leader of the Yeti clan. He has acquired many powers through prolonged and severe meditation."

"For centuries, the Yetis have been trying to rule this region. We have been fighting them and protecting our land, because we know that if they overpower us, they will destroy all humanity. There are many secrets hidden in this land. These secrets have been protected by the inhabitants of these mountains, for centuries. They have confided in us with these secrets and now it is our duty to protect them. The Yetis with their bad intentions could never get the secrets."

"But King Yeti refused to give up. So he went underground to perform a meditation that would make him invincible. For years he was buried deep inside the snow, surrounded and protected by the powerful meditation circle. I wonder how you could enter the 'Forbidden Circle'! Not to mention, you distracted him from his age old meditation. It is difficult to believe how you are still alive. There must be some powerful force that is protecting you."

"You are right," said Steve, "the great force that protects us all the time is our grandmaster."

"Your grandmaster?" asked the creature. "Who is your grand master?"

"My grandmaster belongs to the sacred land of India. He is the leader of a Gompa—a Buddhist monastery at the foothills of the Himalayas." said Steve.

"I request you to tell me your master's name." said the creature.

"No, we are not supposed to take our Master's name," said Steve, loud and clear.

"It's important for all of us," the creature insisted.

"I can't," was Steve's defiant answer.

"I implore you to tell me your master's name"

said the creature. "If he is the grandmaster from Gompa in the Himalayas, I must know his name. This might change everything right now."

"Shom!" was Steve's short reply.

At the mention of Shom's name, the creature took a few hurried steps backwards. He stood there looking deep into the eyes of Steve, as if searching for something within them. An uneasy silence fell over the place; no one moved.

Steve was confused and watched the creature closely. He felt that those glittering blue eyes were swimming in a few drops of water. And a drop of water trickled down his snowy check. "Is he weeping?" thought Steve, "but why should he weep?

And the creature replied to his thoughts. "What have I done?" The Viola leader's eyes were filled with remorse. "How could I make such a big mistake?" Then, he waved his hand in the air. Within seconds, hundreds of ice warriors came and stood before him. The creature waved both hands and seemed to be speaking to the warriors in some kind of sign language. The next moment the soldiers turned into tiny snow globules and rolled over to cover the bodies of Steve and Cheeka. As if by magic, both the boys were freed from their bondage. They ran and hugged each other. Soon the violet web rays disappeared for a moment and Pinkoo was free. She flew and hugged the nose of both her friends. All three were united at last. The creature watched them silently. Then he floated in air and came close to them.

"Brother," he addressed Steve.

Steve was taken aback. "Why do you call me bother now?" He asked.

"Do not misunderstand me, bother," said the creature remorsefully. "We are like brothers because we are disciples of the same grandmaster. If we exist today, it is because of our master's protective blessing and guidance. He has been guiding me and my clan for years. I thank God that this truth about you and our grandmaster was revealed to me before it was too late. If I only knew this, you would never have gone through this trouble. We are indeed very sorry, brother." As he said this, the entire clan of warriors walked up to Steve and his friends and laid their weapons at their feet. Steve was taken aback.

"Oh, no-no...please! You don't need to do this. I realize that you had to capture us because we were trespassing. Had we not come to this land, had we not bumped into the Yeti King, had we not tripped and fallen into your cave, all this would not have happened," Steve said with a sad heart.

"Oh yes, I should have thought of that earlier," said the leader of the clan. "But tell me brother, how did you land into this trouble?"

"It's a long story," he said, "the past one week has been full of incidents. It seems like an experience of several years."

"Your eyes tell me the story of long pain and struggle," said the creature. "But please tell me what brought you to this land? Was it our grandmaster's desire? Is he alright?"

"He's caught in a terrible condition," said a teary-eyed Steve. The thought of the deep anguish and pain that his master must be suffering, filled him with sadness.

"What has happened to our master? Please tell me everything in detail. I am worried," said the creature, looking visibly concerned.

Steve narrated all the incidents that led them to Alaska. An uneasy silence took over the place. The horror unleashed by Kapaal in the peaceful land of the Gompa filled the creature's eyes with tears. "Oh, my good Lord!" he sighed. "Why did this have to happen to our master? And innocent kids like you and your friends had to go through such pain!"

The creature and his clan listened to Steve in rapt attention, as he continued to tell them that he was here in pursuit of the first of the seven paintings—the Violet painting. That's when Pinkoo butted in with, "We've got to find the violet painting and then the six remaining paintings." Then she added turning to their leader, "Can you please help us?"

"It is my duty and the duty of our Viola clan to do everything we can, for you. In fact, I feel that this land was chosen to hide the violet painting because it belongs to our Viola tribe. We are called the Viola tribe because we are born of the violet light. You must have noticed that there are violet rays all around us. Violet is our lifeline, Violet is our power. The Violet painting would be most secure in our land."

"We have a map that can show us the location of the painting," said Cheeka.

"But...I think we lost it during our accidental fall into this cave," said Steve, feeling unsure.

Pinkoo was shocked to hear this and wondered

how they would continue with their expedition!

"Nothing gets lost in Viola land," said the leader. "My soldiers had found it and have taken good care of your map."

He pointed his fingers toward the floor gestured something, as if communicating to the space around him. Out of thin air emerged a violet colored symbol, floating mid-air. Then the violet rays emitting from his finger tips pushed the symbol onto the floor. Before the awestruck eyes of the kids the map came out of the floor and attached itself to the violet symbol. The creature made another gesture with his finger and the symbol disappeared leaving the map floating in front of them. The map was fresh and alive as ever.

Steve walked to the map to take a closer look. The land, the sea, the desert, the rivers—continued to be clearly animated. However, the mountain range of Alaska looked hazy. The mountain seemed to be covered with thick snow and there was mist all over. Strangely, the violet spot that was depicting the violet painting in the map earlier was not visible now. But somewhere in the center of the mountains there was an open space that appeared like a valley. Right in the middle of this valley was a shining golden spot. This was a new addition to the map and Steve could not make anything out of it. "Do you recognize the golden spot?" he asked Cheeka.

"No. I can't recollect having seen this spot on the map." he replied.

"This may be something that is related to these people" whispered Pinkoo into Steve's ear.

"You are right little one" said the leader, giving Pinkoo a shock.

"Oh God!" whispered Pinkoo again. "How did he...?"

"Shh!" signaled Steve. "He knows everyone's minds. He reads our thoughts."

"But he doest know my name," said Pinkoo, "he called me little one, just now!"

"You are right again, little one!" said the creature smiling. "I can read your thoughts. But if you don't tell me your name, how will I know?"

"If you can read my thought, then I will not 'tell' my name. I will 'think' my name." said Pinkoo.

"So be it, little one!" said the creature.

"You have given me and my friends enough trouble," thought Pinkoo, "why should I give away my name so easily. And, by the way, why haven't you told us your name?"

"I am really very sorry little one, for all the trouble you have gone through," said the creature. Everyone here calls me Grand-brother. Should I call you Little Sister?"

Pinkoo stared at Grand-brother in amazement. "You can really read our thoughts," she said. "I thought only our grandmaster had this power."

"It is through his blessings and training that I have acquired this power, little one," said Grand-brother. "Now tell me, do I call you Little Sister, or by some other name?"

"Well, I am Pinkoo, and these are my friends Steve and Cheeka," said Pinkoo.

"We are confused, Grand-brother," said Steve

who was still puzzled by the new addition to the map. "The spot that indicated the location of the Violet painting in the map has disappeared. In its place stands a golden spot. Can you explain why?"

Grand-brother looked at the map. He closed his eyes and started meditating. Gradually a spot in the center of his forehead started to emit a violet beam that seemed to scan the map. When the scanning beam reached the golden spot, a golden star appeared there.

Grand-brother opened his eyes and smiled. "You are lucky, Steve. This is the auspicious Golden Star that appears only once every year. And this is that time of the year. This great star will lead you to your painting. But it is not as easy as it sounds."

Steve, Cheeka and Pinkoo listened attentively as Grand-brother continued. "The great Golden Star is visible only for a few minutes. You have to grab it as soon as it appears. I say 'grab it' because I have a feeling that you are not the only person who is looking for it. There are other greedy hands that want to grab it. Don't forget the Yeti clan and their King. For ages, they have wanted to rule this land. The Golden Star could lead them to the Violet painting and then to the Creatures of the Rainbow!"

"For the first time in history these paintings have come out of their secure abode in the Gompa," Grand brother went on. "Like the greedy and evil Kapaal, many other evil forces will be eyeing those powerful paintings. So Steve, my brother, now you know what lies ahead of you."

"All I know is that I am on a mission given to me

by my grand master. And with the help of my friends Cheeka and Pinkoo, I will fulfill it one day!" said Steve with determination.

"And our grandmaster is with us always," reminded Cheeka. "He has been protecting us and will take care of us until we accomplish our task."

"My grandmaster has given me the responsibility of my friends and I will never let them down!" added innocent Pinkoo.

To this Grand-brother added, "Consider us a part of your mission. Our grandmaster is in trouble and we will do everything possible to help you."

"Without your help we will not be able to do anything, Grand-brother," said Steve. "Please guide us."

"Of course, we are all one in this mission!" said Grand-brother. "Now, the first thing to consider is where the Golden Star will appear. It is far from here and the terrain is rough. It will not be easy to reach the place. Secondly, we have less than twenty four hours to get there. The Golden Star will appear at midnight tomorrow and you will have just a few minutes to grab it. So forget sleep, forget hunger. We have to get started right away!"

Grand-brother waved his fingers in the air and produced another floating violet symbol. All the tiny soldiers present in the cave gestured to produce many more such violet symbols. Within moments, hundreds of symbols were floating across the cave as if a message was being sent across. Soon thousands of snow globules crawled toward Steve, Cheeka and Pinkoo. The globules started covering their body.

The kids were startled. Grand-brother realized this and pacified them. "Don't worry, you will not be hurt. We have to venture into the bitter cold. They are preparing you for that."

Within a few moments Steve, Cheeka and Pinkoo's bodies were totally covered with snow globules. Soon the globules started receding down their body; revealing warm fur coats that now covered the kids.

"That's better," said Grand-brother. Then he turned toward the Viola clan and addressed them. "Friends, we need to set out on the most important mission of our lives. Let us make it absolutely clear in our minds that this is not a mere journey. It's a mission that becomes all the more important because it involves our grandmaster and three friends who are very precious to us. I want all of you to be aware that the path to the valley of the Golden Star is not only difficult, but is also filled with danger at every step. We might be encountering natural calamities or man-made obstructions. But let this not deter us from our mission. The Golden Star has to be in the hands of our friends at any cost."

Grand-brother then turned to Steve. "Brother Steve, we pledge all our support to you and your friends. But there are certain things that you need to remember. The valley of the Golden Star has a circle in its center which is called the "Forbidden Circle". This is the rarest piece of land on earth, unknown to the rest of humanity. It is because of this circle that the earth remains in its orbit. Every planet in our solar system has a similar 'Forbidden Circle'. This is an area that connects the planets to each other and to the supreme power of the sun. Scientists and astronomers keep working on theories, but there are numerous celestial secrets that are yet to be discovered. Some wonders are created by God and we humans can't understand them."

Steve, Cheeka, and Pinkoo listened on in amazement, but were not able to completely comprehend what he said.

"Let this not distract you, my friend," continued Grand-brother. "I had to mention the "Forbidden Circle" because you have to take extreme caution before entering it. This is an area where the gravitational pull is stronger than anywhere else. It is at this spot that the gravitational force of all the planets and the sun in focused. Anyone who steps into this area will get pulled by tremendous force, to the center of the earth. His body weight will increase many times and taking a single step ahead can drain all his energy. If a person remains within the circle too long, he will be pulled to the heart of the earth and will perish."

This was a frightening thought. Steve noticed Cheeka and Pinkoo staring at him. But, right now Steve wanted to think about the task at hand. "What about the Golden Star?"

"I am coming to that," said Grand-brother. "The Golden Star will appear at midnight, exactly at the center of the 'Forbidden Circle'. This is the only time of the year when the gravitational power of this area becomes normal—I mean, similar to the gravitation in other places. That will be your chance to enter the circle. But this chance will last for just a few minutes. These few precious moments will last as long as the Golden Star will be on earth. This is when you have to use all your strength to run toward the Golden Star and grab it."

"Remember, the Golden Star will disappear as fast as it will appear. Once it disappears, the gravitational power inside the 'Forbidden Circle' will increase tremendously, and everyone inside the circle will perish, except us. We, the soldiers of the Viola Tribe have been gifted the power of turning into snow balls. We will merge into the snow and come out of the circle."

Grand-brother turned to his soldiers. "It's time for us to make preparations to come out of our cave and start our journey toward the valley."

All the ice soldiers gathered near their leader. He signaled to them and they made a circle around Steve and his friends. He closed his eyes and folded his hands in a gesture of meditation. As he meditated, the violet gem on his forehead started to glow. Gradually he raised both his hands toward the ceiling.

"Brother…!" Steve could hear Grand-brother speaking to him through his thoughts. "Please hold each other tightly, and do not let go until I ask you to."

"Yes Grand-brother," said Steve and held Cheeka's hand, while Pinkoo took refuge in his pocket.

Everyone looked up at the ceiling. The violet rays emitting out of Grand-brother's hands were spreading like thick violet clouds on the ceiling of the cave. Gradually, the clouds started revolving. Out of nowhere a strong wind gushed into the cave and started circulating. The wind moved in the direction of the clouds, thus adding to their speed. Now, the walls of the cave also started rotating in sync with the movement of the wind and clouds. The circular movement inside the cave gained tremendous momentum. The wind and clouds rotating at top speed started creating a tornado of sorts. Steve had heard of twisters and here was one right in front of his eyes. Such was the power of the wind that he was feeling breathless. The mist created by the tornado was blurring his vision. He could hardly see anything. Even Cheeka seemed to disappear in front of his eyes. He clutched tightly to Cheeka's hand. Soon, his feet were swept off the ground and he realized that it was not due to the powerful wind, but because of lack of gravity inside the cave. In fact, it did not appear like a cave anymore. The rotating walls and the ceiling made the structure appear like a huge space ship. Steve and Cheeka were now floating mid-air.

"Hey, Cheeka!" said Steve. "Are you feeling the same as me?"

"I am floating!" shouted Cheeka in excitement, "and I see you are floating too."

"But I am not floating," said Pinkoo peeking out of Steve's pocket, "let me try."

"Absolutely not!" screamed Steve, "you will disappear in this tornado. Just stay put!" said Steve, pushing her back into his pocket.

"How selfish!" grumbled Pinkoo. "Why should

boys have all the fun?"

The activity in the cave kept increasing in intensity. The huge structure was being lifted from inside the earth to above the ground. While Steve and Cheeka were struggling to not get swayed away from each other, the ice soldiers were firmly stuck to snow on the floor.

Steve saw Cheeka fumbling for something inside his fur coat. "What are you looking for?"

"It's the map," replied Cheeka. "I am not sure where I had kept it."

"This is not to time for it, Cheeka. Let things settle down. I am sure everything is in place," said Steve.

But Cheeka was worried about the map. After groping for sometime, he found something. In a hurry, he drew it out of his coat to ascertain that it was the map. And in this hurry he committed the biggest mistake of his life. The strong wind snatched the map away from his hand. The map flew at lightening speed and got sucked into the twister. Cheeka panicked and lunged toward the map without realizing that leaving Steve's hand could be fatal for him. Before Steve could realize what was happening, he had lost his grip on Cheeka. Chasing the map, Cheeka dived toward the twister and got swallowed in, along with Steve's screams, "No, Cheeka...No!"

Cheeka had disappeared inside the twister. As far as Steve was concerned, there was neither time nor choice. But Grand-brother warned him about following Cheeka. "Have patience, brother! We will save him." But nothing could stop Steve from saving his companion. Without a second thought, he plunged into the twister and was lost out of sight.

Inside the twister was a volcano of energy. This was the tremendous energy that was buoying up the cave toward the ground above it. Flying at the speed of sound, Steve was still in his senses. He looked around. There was no sign of Cheeka. The energy created by the tremendous movement of the wind and the clouds created sparks of lightning inside the twister. Anything hit by the flash of fire would be charred in an instant. Steve was using all his energy to keep afloat and save himself from the lightening. Suddenly he got a glimpse of his friend. Like a flash Cheeka appeared before him, then disappeared. In that fraction of a second, Steve could make out that Cheeka was unconscious. Steve cried out. "Please help, Master. Please save us!"

Inside the Gompa, all the monks were in silent meditation. A flash of lightening broke their silence. Everyone opened their eyes and saw the image of their grandmaster Shom floating in front of them.

"Listen carefully," the grandmaster spoke. "Our friends are in trouble. Your chanting can save them. I urge you to waste no time and start right now." Shom's image faded out, and the very next moment the meditation room was reverberating with chants. The chanting grew louder. A careful observer would have been able to see a hint of the sound waves traveling through the snow capped Himalayas. In a matter of seconds, the sound waves reached the heart of the twister, inside the cave. And another miracle was accomplished.

A new tornado grew inside the twister and started rotating in the opposite direction. A powerful gust of energy rose upward and blasted a hole in the huge ceiling of the cave. At an unbelievable speed both the twisters swept through the hole, taking the boys along with them and throwing them outside the cave, into the open land. With dwindling vision, Steve saw Cheeka being flung out with him. And then it was all black.

There was pin-drop silence inside the meditation hall of the Gompa. The chanting was over and everyone waited to know if the kids were fine.

"They are safe," assured Shom's voice, as his image reappeared before them. "Please pray for their recovery. They will continue to need our support." Shom's image vanished again, and the group began their healing meditation.

*

JOURNEY TO THE GOLDEN STAR

Bright daylight glistened on the white snow. Steve tried to adjust his eyes to the light and also to see through the thick fog that was blurring everything that was in front of him. He could make out the faint outline of Cheeka's body lying beside him.

When he moved closer, Steve was reassured to see Cheeka's tired smile. He quickly felt his pocket and as if on cue Pinkoo peeped out and said, "I must say you guys have become extremely irresponsible. Imagine, grown ups like you, jumping into twisters and getting into big trouble. What a roller-coaster ride that was. I am still giddy."

"Ok! Calm down, little one," said Grand-brother. He and his group were surrounding the kids. Cheeka looked around, his eyes searching for something.

"Is this what you're looking for?" asked Grand-brother, showing the map. Cheeka smiled faintly.

"You need to stop worrying, both of you. Worry is in your mind, which never helps a situation. Worry is a negative feeling created by the mind which colors a situation into a problem. The situation remains as it is, but worry compels you to take panicked measures that worsen the situation. And that's exactly what you did, my friends." said Grand-brother. "I understand and appreciate your concern. But be assured brother, that the Viola tribe shall always protect you and do everything that you need to accomplish your mission."

Steve and his friends listened to Grand-brother attentively. It was a lesson of a life time for them.

"You are right Grand-brother," said Steve. "We have learnt our lesson the hard way." He turned to Cheeka and said, "Let's get on with the map." Cheeka looked at the map. A narrow path leading to the Golden Star was faintly visible. However, there was a dark black spot on top of the mountain, and it kept blinking. "This black spot was not there earlier. What could it be and why is it blinking."

"I think your map is indicating some unforeseen danger. It's a warning of some sort. Right now, it would be difficult to guess what it is. We will know for sure only when we reach the mountains," said Grand-brother, now appearing a bit concerned.

He turned to his soldiers and addressed them. "This map indicates a hidden path the west, to the Golden Star. We first need to find that path."

Grand-brother looked at the snow that spread for miles ahead of him. There was no sign of a path. Steve and Cheeka looked around, but could see nothing more than vast expanse of snow. The ice soldiers stood still, waiting for orders from Grand-brother. An uneasy silence fell over the place, which was broken by the occasional noise of the sharp winds blowing.

"Hey look! I can clearly see the route through the map!" Pinkoo said in an exciting voice.

Everyone jerked at the sudden interjection.

"Where are you Pinkoo?" asked Steve.

"Up here," said Pinkoo. Everyone looked up and saw Pinkoo floating along with the map.

"You are smarter than I thought, little one," said Grand-brother. "How did you manage to take the map up there?"

"I asked it to help me and it just came along," said Pinkoo, smiling. Everyone was amused.

"Hey, Steve!" she continued. "I think you know how to use this map. You can find the path for us."

Steve understood what she was trying to say. He raised his right hand toward the sun. As the sunrays touched his hand, a beautiful rainbow emerged from his palm and passed into the map. The map was immediately vibrant with the colors that spread across its length and breadth. Somewhere on the other end of the map the seven colors re-converged into the dazzling ray of the sun. This strong beam hit the ground below. The entire group watched in amazement as the brilliant light coming out of the map paved its way through the snow. As it dashed ahead, the snow around instantly melted and gave way, revealing an idyllic path leading to the mountain.

There were smiles on all the faces, as Pinkoo flew down with the map. Steve and Cheeka gave her a loving hug.

Grand-brother patted her on her cute little wing. "You have done a great job! We are proud of you."

Pinkoo pulled up the collar of her new feather coat, put on the golden crown presented by the queen of butterflies and looked around with pride.

"Well friends, no time to waste; let's march on." Grand-brother took the lead and the party followed. They moved on with hopes in their hearts, unaware of careful eyes that watched every move from up in the sky.

Although his evil master was trapped in a mirror maze, Kapaal's bat had not lost sight of Steve. It was now time for this loyal messenger to report the latest. The bat flew to a barren thorny bush. Hanging upside down on a branch, he transmitted high frequency sound waves that penetrated through all objects and entered the mirror maze inside the Gompa.

The ultra sonic waves touched Kapaal's shaft. The diamond on the tip of the shaft started to glow. Kapaal opened his eyes with a jolt. His ears turned toward the ultra sonic sound, and like a transmitter he started receiving signals from the bat.

He could clearly hear the nervous voice of his 'pet.' "Master...Master!"

"Stop panicking, you fool!" an irritated Kapaal communicated through super sonic sound waves emitting from the diamond of his shaft.

"Pardon me master, but they are moving west toward the mountains. Their magic map had made an easy path for them. If all goes right, they will reach the valley of the Golden Star before time." The bat's voice was quivering as he said this.

"It's a 'Big If,' my dear disciple. Remember, a 'big if' can make any action questionable. A 'big if' can make any journey 'impossible.' And I am the 'impossible' factor in their journey. Do you think a handful of kids and a bunch of pygmies can achieve what I—the greatest 'Kapaal' cannot achieve? I shall crush them before they reach the top of the mountains. Are you ready for it?"

"Yes, my Lord. Command me." asked the bat nervously.

"I know a person who will dig their watery graves. He is the gurgling witch doctor, Goya, an old friend. Just go to him and he will take care of everything.

"But where can I find him, master?"

"Simple, my evil boy," chuckled Kapaal. "Just watch out for the Red Lotus in the mystical pond, on the eastern foothills of the mountains. Now, go!"

On the western route, where the party had made good progress, Grand-brother suddenly stopped. The others, who were behind him, came to a halt.

"What is it, Grand-brother?" inquired Steve.

Grand-brother kept quite, closed his eyes. It looked like he was concentrating on something. His fluffy, cloud-like fur contracted as he stood still, trying to feel something. After a while he broke his silence. "An activity in the east makes me uneasy," he said. "I receive messages of sabotage."

The whole group watched in silence as Grand-brother rose from the ground and floated in air.

"Our grand master warns us of evil forces that may disrupt our mission." Grand-brother raised both his hands as he spoke. "Friends, let it be known to all of us that we are here for a great cause. We are on a mission of service to humanity, to save our planet. We are on the path of God and no one...no one can stop us. Remain united, remain close to one another and be of support; no matter what the eventuality. May God be with all of us! Let's move now!"

The group moved on with some premonition in their hearts. But little did they know about the scale of danger lurking behind them.

At the eastern end, a black bat was flying restlessly, in search of the Red Lotus. In the huge expanse of snow that spread for miles, a pond was beyond imagination. After a while, he got exhausted and perched himself upside down on a thorny branch. Hanging from the branch he looked around.

"Where on earth can I find a pond in the middle of this frozen land?" he wondered, feeling hopeless. Just then, his attention was drawn to a mirror-like spot glistening at the foothill of the mountain.

"Is it...?" he thought, and flew toward the shining spot. But as he went near the area, the shining spot disappeared. He was sure he had seen the spot and was flying in the right direction. Disappointed, he looked around and soon saw the glistening spot in another area. He flew toward it. But before he could reach the spot, it disappeared and appeared in another area. This sequence of events repeated itself several times.

Exhausted and frustrated, the bat went back to his thorny branch. Hanging upside down, he closed his eyes and thought, "Why is this happening to me? Is it some mystical experience?"

"No! It's a punishment!" It was "Master!" the bat said in a shock. "Why this punishment? What have I done?"

"How could you start on a mission without worshiping me?" commanded Kapaal.

"I am indeed very sorry, my Lord," said bat remorsefully.

"Then say, 'Hail Kapaal!" commanded Kapaal.

"HAIL KAPAAL!" shouted the bat in fear and awe.

"Repeat!" came Kapaal's command again.

"Hail Kapaal!" repeated the bat.

"Again," ordered Kapaal

"Hail Kapaal!"

"Now open your eyes," was the next order.

The bat opened his eyes to see that right below the branch from which he was hanging was a bright red lotus, in the middle of a small pond. The deep blue water of the pond was shimmering in the bright sunlight. "How could the water remain liquid in the middle of a land covered with snow?" wondered the bat.

"My Lord! You are great!" said on overwhelmed bat. "Only you could create such an illusion. The Red Lotus is right below this branch. What do I do now?"

"Ha-ha-ha! Illusions and Miracles are a part of Kapaal's life," said the evil man with pride. "Now what are you waiting for, stupid? Just go and snatch the lotus."

The bat hesitated for a while. He knew that there is some black mystery in every illusion that Kapaal creates.

"What are you waiting for?" boomed Kapaal's voice.

"Well, nothing actually..." said the nervous bat.

"Then just go for it, you fool." shouted Kapaal.

The bat had no choice but to obey his master. He dived at the Red Lotus. As he dug his blood-sucking fangs into the Red Lotus he thought, "Never mind that this is not blood. As least I will enjoy the sweet nectar of the Red Lotus." The bat sucked hard at the lotus' center and suddenly stopped! "I can't believe this!" he thought and sucked harder. He stopped again in disbelief.

"My Good Lord!" he thought. "How can I even thank you? This is pure blood! You knew how hungry I've been."

Hearing no response, the bat pinched himself to ensure that he was in his senses. How can a lotus possibly have blood inside it? He went on sucking greedily, drinking to his heart's content.

What he didn't realize was that as the blood got sucked out, the color of the Red Lotus was fading its color and its petals were growing larger. Gradually, the blood-red lotus became white. Its enlarged petals now looked like the ears of an elephant.

Unaware of his surroundings, the bat enjoyed the blood flowing into his fangs. He sucked and sucked, until the last drop of blood was gone. The contented bat looked around in amazement, feeling a bit tipsy.

Now, the lotus was absolutely snow white and ten times larger than its original size. "Hey! Wasn't this lotus red in color?" he said to himself.

"You are right."

The shocked bat looked around to see where the answer came from. But he could spot no one.

"It's me, the lotus you are sitting on," said the lotus.

"You can talk too!" said the bat, now a little alarmed. "How did you turn white and so big?"

"Because you sucked all my blood," said the lotus.

"But I have not heard of a lotus with blood instead of nectar."

"Well, what were you suckling at merrily, you greedy little creature?" asked the lotus.

"It tasted like blood." said the bat "It was blood. But not my blood," said the lotus, quite matter-of-factly.

"Not your blood?" asked the bat in fear.

"You see, you're not the only one who was lured by my lovely red color!" said the lotus, sounding rather proud of her cunning intentions. "My color has proven to be a fatal attraction for many a creature. They end up here, having their last drop of nectar."

"Do you mean that you are...?" said the confused bat.

"You guessed it right, you greedy bat! I am a blood-sucking lotus!" With this last statement, the huge petals of the lotus started closing in on the bat.

The bat struggled to fly off, but his feet were stuck to the sticky surface of the lotus. He could not move. When the large petals shut over him, the bat screamed, "Hey! Hold on; this is not fair!"

"And you think it was fair when you drank 'my' blood?" resorted the lotus.

"Well, eh...I was hungry...and...thirsty." The bat's reasoning was clearly not working with the lotus.

"Well, I am thirsty all the time. Ha-ha-ha!" The eerie laughter echoed within the petals that were tightened over the bat. Soon, small sharp needles came out of the petals.

The bat was overcome with such immense fear that he could only manage a squeak. "Are you trying to kill me?"

"No, I am trying to play soccer with you. He-he!" chuckled the lotus.

"This is no time for jokes," said the trembling bat. "You can't kill me. I am on a mission."

"Most animals make this excuse before they die. Do you have a last wish, eh?" said the disinterested lotus.

"Yes! I want to meet Goya—the gurgling witch doctor," the bat said hurriedly.

Suddenly the grip of the petals loosened. "What did you say?" "I want to meet Goya—the gurgling witch doctor," repeated the bat. "Who told you about him?" asked the Red Lotus, a bit bewildered. "My grandmaster—Kapaal," replied the bat. "Why did you not tell this before?" asked the lotus in bewilderment. "You did not give me a chance," said the bat meekly.

"Ok, ok! Let's not argue," said the lotus as he opened out his petals. The needles were pulled back into the petals.

"Don't worry now. I won't harm you. Just come with me." The Red Lotus covered the bat with her petals and dived into the pond. With the bat inside of her, she swam deep into the blue waters under the snow. After swimming for a while she came up to the surface and opened her petals.

The bat looked around. It was a dome made of ice, partly transparent, partly opaque. Sunlight filtered through the transparent part, revealing the shape of the place. "What spooky place is this?" whispered the bat to himself.

As he sat on the Red Lotus, floating on the water, he looked up to find skulls hanging from the ceiling. Skulls of different shape and size; skulls that were once part of humans, animals, and birds. Lizards, cockroaches, and insects had made their homes inside the skulls. A lizard jumped to eat a cockroach, but slipped off from the skull and fell into the water. Surprisingly, its body got charred and turned into ash in a few minutes. That was when the bat realized that the Red Lotus was not floating on water. It was probably some kind on an acid. The bat noticed multi-colored bubbles appearing on the surface of the liquid. Yet, huge blocks of ice floated on this boiling surface. On these ice blocks, lay skeletons of animals and humans.

The bat was lost in these sights, when the Red Lotus screamed, "What are you staring at? You have come to meet our master, Goya, haven't you?"

"Yes. Oh yes! I forgot..." The bat had still not regained his senses. "So call him," the Red Lotus interjected. "Yes, of course." The bat gathered all his courage and called out "Goya! Goya!"

Thud came down a petal, like a slap on his back. "Are you out of your mind?" said the annoyed lotus. "He is our master. The king of this land! Address him with respect."

"Very sorry!" said the bat. Then, he shouted out again, "Your Highness! Master of all the gurgling witch doctors! King of the land of gurgling acid! I beseechingly request you to make your kind appearance and help your humble servant." Having said all of this in one breath, the bat waited.

Soon large bubbles started to surface at the center of the acid land. The bubbles soon grew in number and size, creating a fountain of bubbles. This was followed by a gurgling sound which increased with the size of the bubble fountain. The gurgling sound grew so loud that it echoed all around the dome. The bubbles were followed by thick gray smoke. The smoke spread all around. Then from under the bubbling acid emerged a figure. The bat tried to see, but the thick smoke blurred his vision. He was wondering how the strange creature would look. How would he talk? How would he react? He mustered all his courage and finally spoke. "Are you Goya?"

"GURGGLE...!" with a large gurgling sound the creature spat a thick liquid fireball toward the bat.

As he dodged the fireball, the bat realized his mistake, and said, "Am I the fortunate creature to see the grand appearance of His Majesty, King of the land of gurgling acid—Lord Goya?"

"Gurgle - gurgle...You have still not seen me," came a deep, but hollow voice from behind the smoke. "So why lie?"

"Sorry, your Heaviness...I mean...Your Highness!" said the bat, now more nervous than before, "but I am keen to see you."

"Gurgle - gurgle - gurgle.... (SPIT)!" The creature spat another ball of liquid fire and immediately the smoke cleared. From behind the smoke, appeared a horrid looking creature with the face of a fat man and the body of a frog. Each of his eyes had two eyeballs that rotated in opposite direction. The face was greased with oil. Thick drops of perspiration seemed to be a permanent feature on the forehead. The mouth was broad and extended from one ear to the other. A green, slithering tongue kept hanging out permanently. The body was like a bulky toad with a green skin and a fat yellow stomach. The whole body was covered with shiny green scales, resembling those of a fish. Behind him followed a thin thorny tail that moved constantly across the back of his body like a wiper on the windscreen of a car.

Goya did not seem to care about the bat's presence. The four eye balls moved in different directions, as if searching for something. Then, he found it. His tongue sprang out of his mouth, stretched out more than twenty meters, and caught a giant spider on the ceiling. The tongue jerked back into his mouth and Goya swallowed the huge spider in one gulp.

"Gurgle - gurgle," said Goya, smacking his lips. "Oh! I was starving."

The bat looked at him fearfully. "Yes sir. In fact, you deserve much more than this." He didn't know why he was saying all this. Probably he was trying to overcome his nervousness. "So Blacky, (gurgle) what brings you here?" said Goya. "My grand master, Kapaal, said only you could help me," said the bat meekly.

"You are my friend Kapaal's disciple? (Gurgle) You should have told me earlier. I was about to (gurgle - gurgle) have you for lunch. You are a well fed bat, Blacky! I like you." said Goya rolling his green tongue over his lips and pushing one left-over hairy leg of the spider into his mouth.

"Hee-hee..." The bat tried his best to smile while his knees were trembling. "My Lord! The Gurggling King. We don't have much time in hand. We need your help!" "Well, what is the issue?" asked Goya. The bat narrated the entire story as precisely as he could, finally adding, "The party is advancing fast. We have got to stop them before they cross the mountains."

"Gurgle - gurgle ...... Ha-ha ...... ha-ha. Gurgle - gurgle...he-he!" Goya gurgled and laughed and croaked for what seemed to last a couple of minutes. "Why are you so worried Blackie? This is a trifle for Goya. They will never be able to cross 'my' mountain. If they try, they will perish!"

*

THE IMPENDING DANGER

Unaware of the Goya's intentions, Grand-brother was steadily leading his team toward their mission. They had reached the foothills of the mountain. Steve looked up at the majestic mountain covered with snow and wondered how he would he able to climb it. He looked at Cheeka who smiled back at him.

"I have never climbed a mountain, have you?" he asked Cheeka.

"Some hills," said Cheeka, "but not such a huge mountain. And we have no equipments to climb."

"Wish I could fly like you, Pinkoo!" said Steve.

"But this doesn't look too easy for me either," said Pinkoo.

"Why do you worry when Grand-brother is with you," said Grand-brother smiling at them. He signaled to all the members of the Viola tribe. "Friends, now begins the difficult part of our journey. The only way we can reach the top is by becoming one with the snow. Our brothers do not have the means to climb. So we will become their steps. Are you with me?"

"Always, Grand-brother," came the chorus.

Grand-brother smiled and made a violet symbol in the air. With the wind, the symbol passed over every member of the group. Steve and Cheeka felt as if tiny violet crystals were raining over them. Pinkoo peeped out, caught a couple of crystals and hid them inside Steve's pocket. The crystals had a calming effect on everyone. It filled the kids with confidence and courage.

"This will protect you from all dangers," said Grand-brother. Then, turning to Steve, he said, "And remember, that the path you have chosen is God's gift to you. You are on this mission because God feels you are special. So have faith and face everything that comes your way. God will always protect you." Then like a war cry he called out, "Let's go!"

While Steve and Cheeka were still wondering how to start the climb, the ice soldiers turned into snow globules once again. The globules then started merging together to form a block of ice.

"Now, that's your first step," said Grand-brother. "Please step on it."

Steve and Cheeka climbed on the block, by which time another block was formed above it. One by one, block by block the boys started climbing the mountain. No one had the slightest idea of what was being conspired behind their back.

Inside his den, Goya was preparing for a large-scale assault. The bat was watching him in awe. With his long tongue, Goya plucked out five skulls from the ceiling. An owl's skull that had a family of cockroaches inside it, a pig's skull that was the hideout for a rat, a frog's skull that had frog eggs laid inside it, a lizard's skull nesting a beehive, and finally, a human skull that had a live human heart throbbing inside it.

Having collected the skulls along with animals and insects resident in them, Goya dumped them all into an ancient copper cauldron. The old rusted pot looked exquisite. It had images of all the planets of the solar system engraved on it, along with the sun in the center. Goya put both his hands into the cauldron and started to crush the skulls along with the animals and insects within them. His fingers were working like a grinder crushing and squeezing everything. As a paste was being made inside, the rust on the cauldron disappeared and the copper began to shimmer like it was new. Goya then took a deep breath and held it. A couple of minutes passed by and Goya did not breathe out. The bat watched as Goya's face gradually turned red and his nostrils spread wide. Even then Goya did not let go of his breath. Smoke started coming out of his nostrils and ear. Goya continued to hold his breath. His face started swelling, turned crimson, and looked like it was about to burst. Finally, Goya spat a big lump of molten fire ball into the cauldron.

The bat shrank to the corner of a petal on the lotus, as he watched the frightful sight. The moment the liquid fire ball fell into the cauldron, it mixed with the pulp of skulls. That spurred a sudden burst of activity within the cauldron. On the exterior of the pot, the planets and the sun came alive and started moving in their orbits. Within the cauldron, the contents started to boil. It appeared as if a fountain of fire was erupting from the base of the pot. The concoction grew in size. Intermittently steaming tentacles of the boiling liquid would reach out from the mouth of the cauldron. The planets on its surface started revolving at a tremendous pace around the sun. The sun was shining like a ball of fire that seemed to be adding to the heat of that huge copper vessel. The liquid inside it started to turn into an angry red color; it looked much like the lava of a volcano. At this point the pot started shaking. Goya watched all this with pride. In his excitement, his body turned orange and he grew bigger in size. His eye balls—all four of them—turned red.

He raised his hands high up into the air and shouted with arrogance, "I summon all the dark forces of this universe to come down to earth. I command that such a power be created inside this pot that it may destroy every creature present on these mountains."

He spat another ball of liquid fire into the pot and instantly a volcano erupted from inside the pot. The red hot lava leaped out of the pot. The moment it touched the acid in the pond, the acid began to evaporate, forming a thick black cloud. The eruption continued; the lava continued to flow. Hundreds and thousands of gallons of acid was being vaporized into clouds—clouds that looked ready to burst.

The bat crouched into his wings, peeping out to see the drama unfold—endless lava pouring out and evaporating gallons of acid into explosive clouds. The ice on the dome started to melt with the heat of the activity. This created a tremor that felt like an earthquake.

Steve and his friends had reached halfway up the mountain, climbing step by step on the ice blocks created by the Viola tribe. At this height, the temperatures had touched below freezing point. It had started to snow and sharp winds were blowing, making their journey difficult. Grand-brother paused for a while and asked Cheeka for the map.

While Grand-brother was studying the map, Steve noticed his expression becoming graver. "Is everything ok?" he asked.

"Everything, except this black spot that is bothering me," said Grand-brother.

Steve saw the map. The black spot that they had seen earlier had grown bigger.

"What does this mean?" asked Cheeka.

"This indicates an extraneous element that could be dangerous." Grand-brother was visibly worried. "But, let this not stop us. We will face it when it shows up. Right now we must focus on our journey. Let's move on."

The party continued with their journey. They were taking every step cautiously when, suddenly, Cheeka slipped on a step and Steve held his hand.

"What happened?" asked Steve.

"I don't know," said Cheeka, "just felt like the ice block shook."

"He is right" said Grand-brother "I can also feel tremors in the mountain. This is not a good sign, because these tremors are unnatural…as if they are man-made. We should try and hurry up. But remember, come what may, we should stay together."

Goya's den withheld the look of an impending disaster waiting to be unleashed. The thick acid clouds had caused cracks on the ice dome. Goya looked gleefully satisfied with his achievement.

"Yes! (Gurgle – gurgle) Yes!" he shouted. "Now is the right time to strike! I order you acid clouds, burst open from this cage and devastate everything on the western end of these mountains. Remember, not even an ant should be spared. GO!"

He spat another huge fireball at the ice ceiling. The molten fire ball burst opened the already cracked ceiling, making way for the clouds to go through. Like a volcano, the smoke gushed through the hole and spread across the sky.

The blast was felt all along the mountain range. Grand-brother, Steve, Cheeka, Pinkoo and all the brave soldiers of the Viola tribe stood still. They were just about fifty meters from the summit. The explosion in the den had shattered the ice blocks. The deep cracks in the steps were threatening to impede their mission.

Cheeka and Steve were standing on separate ice blocks, both of which had almost broken into two pieces. Thankfully, the boys standing on the steps had not fallen. Both of them stood still, not daring to move. Cheeka, who was standing on the upper block gathered courage and extended his hand to Steve.

"Come on, hold my hand and jump onto this

block Steve. Your step might break any moment" said Cheeka.

Steve held Cheeka's hand and was about to jump, when there was another blast.

With the last blast, the cracked step on which Steve was standing gave way. The ice block, which was formed by tiny soldiers, went crumbling down. The broken pieces further disintegrated into ice globules that went rolling down. The globules were trying to unite and form into soldiers, but the speed at which they were falling made it impossible for them to get back to their ice-block form. A few meters down were huge rocks and smashing on those rocks would mean their end. They kept struggling all the way down, and were about to crash, when bright violet rays pierced through them all and held them together. It was Grand-brother. Floating mid-air, he was emitting life saving rays through all his fingers. With their violet lifeline propping them up, the globules started rolling toward each other. They merged back into one another and formed ice soldiers. "Thank you Master! You saved our lives," they said in gratitude.

"I am bound to my duty, my brave soldiers," said Grand-brother. "We shall always be together. Now let's march."

Grand-brother and the ice soldiers quickly rushed to the spot where they had left Steve and his friends. They reached there to find that the boys had been saved by the other soldiers, who had managed to hold on in spite of the blast. Steve and Cheeka were standing on a big block of ice.

"Is everything alright?" asked Grand-brother.

"We are safe as of now," said Steve, "but things don't seem to be alright." He pointed toward the east. A monstrous black cloud had gathered in the sky and was moving toward them. No one had ever seen such a horrifying cloud.

The thick, dark cloud covered a huge expanse in the sky. It seemed to hold some boiling liquid that was emitting smoke all around. The cloud was so huge and heavy that it could not rise high. It remained close to the lower range of the mountains, waiting to burst open. "This is no ordinary cloud. It is not nature's creation. Whoever has created this had evil intentions. And we are the target," said Grand-brother.

There was jubilation inside Goya's den. An unending stream of lava was flowing out of the copper cauldron and merging into the acid, forming an endless stream of acid clouds. The clouds were forming so fast that the acid pond was almost empty. The bat was now hiding behind a rock. Goya was dancing with joy, singing out a tune –

"Ha! gurgle – gurgle – gurgle…
Ho! gurgle – gurgle – gurgle…
'Death' is a beautiful thing…
That's why I like to sing!"

And he roared with laughter, then continued –

"Go evil clouds, and rain – rain – rain;
Dance the 'Rain dance of Death'!
Go – Go – GO!"

The acid clouds were traveling fast toward the west. Grand-brother looked concerned. "If these clouds were to rain here, nothing would survive. We need to move very fast and reach the foothills on the other side of the mountain. Or maybe we could find a shelter. But, we need to do it quickly."

"Where will we find a shelter in this wilderness!" said Steve, desperate by now.

"I have found one!" a jubilant little voice was heard. Pinkoo signaled from a cave within the mountain. The boys' faces brightened up.

"There seems to be enough room in the cave for everyone," said Pinkoo smiling.

"You are our savior, as always!" said Cheeka with tears of happiness.

"But it's quite far;" said Steve, "climbing on blocks takes time. Do we have that much time at hand?"

"There are other ways to the cave," said Grand-brother, and turned to his soldiers. "Friends, listen to me carefully. Divide yourselves into two groups. Arrange yourselves into one huge rectangle on this side and another on that side."

As the ice warriors followed their leader's command, and formed something like a marching formation—one squad on each side. Grand-brother said, "Now Brother Steve and Cheeka lie down on the soldiers."

"But....How could we? Won't they...?" Steve was not able to complete his sentence.

"We have no time to loose," said Grand-brother in urgency. "Trust me, and do as I say."

Each boy climbed on to one squad of soldiers.

And before they could get lied down in their positions, they saw that Grand-brother had transported himself to the cave. From there he extended his hands toward them. Hundreds of violet strings came out of his fingers. "Hold on to the strings," instructed Grand-brother.

The ice soldiers followed and tugged at the strings, which were as strong as mountain climbing ropes. They took on their positions to begin an upward climb, while carrying Steve and Cheeka on their heads.

As they lay on their moving bed of ice soldiers, Cheeka looked up, alarmed at the fast approaching acid cloud.

"Don't look up. Soldiers, pull yourselves upward," shouted Grand-brother.

The soldiers clambered with all their strength. At one end were hundreds of soldiers carrying Steve and Cheeka's weight; at the other end was Grand-brother, all alone. Yet, the party managed to move swiftly.

But the clouds appeared to be approaching faster. As the clouds came nearer, the ground started to tremble. Some soldiers went off balance and Steve slipped off from his position. But they quickly regained their formation.

Inside the den Goya was in his ugliest best. His body had turned red and he had grown into a huge monster. Throwing up his arms in the air he shouted "I summon all the evil forces of the lightning to pierce the acid clouds and explode it. That will make my dream come true!" Lightning flashed across the sky.

The thunder that followed shook the mountains. Grand-brother had closed his eyes in meditation and was drawing all his strength from the Universe to be able to pull the strings. The brave ice soldiers were using all their might to move forward. They were making good progress and would have reached the cave in time. Suddenly the large flash of lightning cut through the violet strings shaking Grand-brother up from his meditation. The boys and the soldiers stood stunned. They were hardly ten meters away from the cave. The clouds were about to rain acid on them. The ominous rumbling of the clouds was tearing the mountains apart.

The ice soldiers lost their grip on the snow and were beginning to slip downwards.

*

LETHAL CLOUDS STRIKE

"This is not good. God, why now?" said Grand-brother, trying not to give up hope. "Friends, only our grand master can save us now."

Steve felt Grand-brother's helplessness. Suddenly, he heard his grandmaster's voice in his heart.

"Why are you in such desperation, my son?" said the voice. "Remember your rainbow, Steve."

Steve looked up. A faint beam of sunlight was visible. It would soon be hidden behind the clouds. Without wasting a moment, he lifted his right palm toward the sun, absorbed all its energies and emitted a bright rainbow toward the cave. Grand-brother and all the ice soldiers watched in amazement as the rainbow spread inside the cave and started buoying the team.

Although the team was moving toward the cave at great speed, the menacing acid cloud was moving faster. The mountain range continued to tremble under the thunder and lightning.

When the team was just about two meters from

the cave, the ugly clouds completely covered the sun and Steve's rainbow disappeared. Thunder rumbled through the mountains and created an avalanche that tumbled toward the group.

Thousands of sparks of lightning pierced the acid clouds. They threatened to burst any moment, charring away everything. Tremendous gusty winds seemed to blow everything away.

"Don't give up for God's sake!" said Grand-brother, at the top of his voice. "You are just a few steps away from your goal. Just believe in yourself and see yourself achieve the end result. Use all your strength and climb up. I know you can do it." Such was the power of the wind and freezing snowfall that Grand-brother's fluffy soft body seemed to disintegrate. But the brave heart leader firmly stood his ground. The boys were totally exhausted by then. With the sun disappearing behind the menacing black cloud Steve seemed to be powerless. How he wished for a glimpse of the sun and his rainbow power would save everyone. Cheeka felt the freezing wind piercing through his warm clothes and entering his bones. But he held to his friend with all his guts. The brave soldiers had started to deform under the tremendous pressure of snow and wind. But they were not ready to give up and made one last attempt. They just lifted the boys on their shoulders and took them up to the cave using every bit of their dwindling energy.

As the last handful of soldiers were getting into the cave, an atomic-explosion-like lightning pierced right through the cloud and burst it into pieces. And hell was let loose. Instead of acid rain, millions of gallons of concentrated acid gushed into the mountain.

Grand-brother saw that about a dozen ice soldiers were stuck under a rock. He rushed to them, covered them with his violet rays and was about to get back into the cave when a huge avalanche struck. There was a total black out inside the cave. The survivors in the cave stood still. The last thing they wanted was to loose Grand-brother.

All along the vast mountain range, the devastation had just begun. Avalanches were let loose. One avalanche followed the other and yet another after another…Hundreds of avalanches came down like monsters. They destroyed every tree, shattered boulders, pieces of which were hurled onto the valley at mindless speeds.

The entrance to the cave was blocked with ice. It was pitch dark inside. Nobody knew how many or who had managed to get in; or how many of them were safe right now.

The noise outside was deafening. Even if someone were to talk aloud, no one would hear him.

An inferno of acid was being played out on the mountain slopes. Thousands of gallons of acid were flowing down. The fiery heat of the acid met the freezing cold of the snow. Amidst harrowing vapors and hissing sounds, miles of snow instantaneously began to boil. The next moment, boiling water mixed with fuming acid, gushed down the mountain destroying everything along the way.

Such destruction had not been seen by anyone before. The mountain was stripped of all its snow. Temperatures that, seconds ago, were below freezing point, had now reached boiling point.

The boiling acid devoured all vegetation and life in the forest at the foot hills. What was beautiful, fragrant, and pleasant, had been turned into ugly, pungent, and desolated. A mindless act of malice had killed thousands of innocent plants, animals, birds, and insects, who had nothing to do with the architects of this destruction.

Mother Nature silently stood watching the inhuman act played out by a mad creature. Was there any justice on this earth to such mindless destruction? Stranded hopelessly in the dark, this thought was overpowering in the hearts of everyone who had survived inside the cave.

At the other end, in the den, Goya—the evil, gurgling witch doctor was thumping his chest victoriously, like King Kong. What a firework he had created! Little did he know that his evil creation was about to be stopped and brought to justice.

The lava erupting from inside the copper vessel kept on flowing. The acid had totally vaporized and the huge pond was dry. Now the lava started filling the pond. Unaware of the impending danger, Goya was busy celebrating. The bat quietly watched the molten fire fill up the pond steadily. He sheepishly began with, "Excuse me, my Lord..."

"Yes, Blackie...gurgle - gurgle. So, finally you

open your mouth (gurgle)!" And with his signature arrogance, Goya continued, "Afraid, are you? Ha-ha…gurgle – gurgle. Ha-ha-ha-ha! Now you have some idea about the power of Goya, eh?

"I am the destructor!" he screamed madly. Every little creature on those mountains has been destroyed! Gurgle – gurgle. Not even a fly can…" He stopped abruptly as he saw a fly struggling to come out of a cobweb. He shot out his long, green tongue and quickly devoured it.

"Slurp…gurgle – gurgle! So what was I saying? Ah, yes! Gurgle – gurgle…not even a fly is left alive. Mission accomplished! Are you happy?" He turned towards the bat as his four eyeballs rotated with excitement.

"Very happy…most obliged, sir," said the bat nervously. "But, my Lord, the…" He was distracted again by the rate at which the level of boiling lava was increasing inside the pond. It looked like the pond would overflow any moment, and the liquid fire would burn the whole place down. He was also terrified by the thought that along with the boys if the map is destroyed, he would have no clue to the paintings. And if this were to happen, his master Kapaal would squeeze him to death.

"What were you saying, Blackie? What is left to say now? Gurgle – gurgle…you selfish bat!" shouted Goya. "I have done so much for you? What are you going to do for me in return, eh?"

"What can a small, useless bat do for you, my Lord?" said the trembling bat.

"You are small, Blackie...but not useless.

Hmm...aren't you...gurgle - gurgle...well fed? How can you be useless? Eh?" said Goya looking at him greedily. "You will be very useful...gurgle - gurgle. A nice juicy meal! After such hard work am I not hungry? Eh...Hee - Hee!"

"W-W-What are you saying...Your Heaviness...I...I mean....Your...High-Highness?" said the bat, dying a hundred deaths that very moment.

"You have heard me right, you nitwit!" said Goya, waving his tongue. "I have given my sweat and breath for you. Now...gurgle - gurgle...I want my pound of flesh." Goya flung his tongue at the bat, which was on alert by then. The bat managed to spring up and dodge Goya's lethal tongue.

"Don't you dare run away from me...you...you insignificant little creature! I will...gurgle - gurgle...gulp you before you know it!" said Goya, as he lashed his tongue furiously at the bat.

But the bat was not waiting to hear his gurgling curses. It flew higher and farther with all his might.

Goya jumped at him without thinking of the consequence. Luckily for the bat Goya narrowly missed him.

"Blow!" shouted Goya as he came down. He looked at the surface under him and realized what a grave mistake he had committed. Just below him was the pond filled with boiling lava. And...'Splash,' he fell into the pond brimming with deadly lava.

As the bat continued to fly, he heard echoes of deathly shrieks. As half of his body turned into ash, the gurgling witch doctor shouted...more in shock, than in agony, "Aaaa - r - gh! Gurgle... Gurgle!

BETRAYAL!" His twenty meter long tongue, tried to whip the bat, but missed narrowly. Even as Goya was dying, he yelled, "I am the King of all I survey! I will not die alone. With me will go down my entire kingdom." He swayed his lethal tongue all around the dome catching every skull, every skeleton, every animal, bird, and insect and putting it all into his large mouth. With so many objects, dead and alive, in his mouth, he could not chew any more. He could not breathe. His face became red and then crimson and finally with a huge blast, it burst into pieces. What remained of him was his long green tongue, which slowly disappeared into the pond of lava.

Goya paid for his evil project with his life, but it was not exactly successful. Although his evil intensions and destructive powers managed to devastate every sight of life in the mountains, they could not touch a handful of noble beings, which were on a divine journey.

The mountains were burning outside. But it was cold and dark inside the cave. The tremendous noise had settled down and there was silence and calm inside.

"Hello! Is anybody around? Please say something. I'm scared," Pinkoo said in a feeble voice. In response to Pinkoo's plea, a violet ray emerged from a corner and spread all over the cave. The ray was emitting from Grand-brother's forehead. It revealed all the faces inside.

"Thank the Lord! Everyone is here—Steve, Cheeka, Grand-brother...and all our friends!" said

Pinkoo as she rushed and hugged Steve and Cheeka.

"We are so happy to see you, little one!" said Steve, kissing her wings.

"Grand-brother, it's only because of you that we've been saved. Thank you…thank you from all of us!" said Cheeka.

"Not at all, my brother," said a teary-eyed Grand-brother. "I have always believed that when you are on a mission of goodness, no evil can touch you. God had saved us. But we are still not out of danger. Because it's cold in here, you have no idea how hot it is out there. Look at the entrance of the cave."

Everyone turned to see that the entrance was covered with a thick wall of solid ice. Grand-brother went up to the entrance and touched the ice. The opacity of the wall cleared to reveal the scene outside. Everything was on fire—the mountains, the trees, the animals and birds. The land that was covered with deep snow had not a drop of water left. Never in the history of humankind had the land of Alaska ever made such a pitiable sight. Everyone had tears in their eyes.

"Our beautiful land has gone forever," said a small ice soldier, in tears.

"The birds will not sing anymore!" said another.

"Where will we butterflies get our nectar from?" said Pinkoo tearfully.

Steve and Cheeka were speechless.

"How will our Viola tribe survive, Grand-brother?" asked a soldier. "We will melt and die in that heat!"

Grand-brother was listening to everyone calmly.

Finally he broke his silence. "Nature is God's creation," he said, "and the creator is always bigger than the destroyer. Nature is meant to heal itself. Haven't you seen trees loose all their leaves and become bear in autumn? But then comes spring and new leaves grow on the same branches. Flowers bloom again and the birds sing. Nothing is permanent. So, if an evil force has destroyed nature and life, it will revive on its own. Change is the law of the universe. And some of us, like Brother Steve here, bring about the change." Grand-brother continued…

"Come, let us join hands and form a circle of Love."

The Viola soldiers formed a tight circle inside the cave. Grand-brother then asked Steve to stand inside the circle. As Steve stood at the center, Grand-brother said, "We will now pray to the Almighty. We will join our good energies together and send it out to the Universe, and ask God to heal nature and all life around."

Grand-brother held Steve's hand and closed his eyes. Everyone held each other's had and stood in silent meditation. After a while, a deep violet halo was formed above Grand-brother's head. Gradually the halo grew in size and reached every member standing in the circle. This energized everyone and each one of them had a halo above them. All the violet halos came together and formed a violet mist that started rising up. The violet mist went through the walls and the ceiling of the cave and spread into the sky. In the presence of the violet mist, all the smoke and dark clouds started disappearing. The calm violet mist covered the sky and soon started raining tiny violet crystals.

The crystals had a magical effect. The fire went off. Everything that was burning cooled down. There was calmness all around. Nature was being healed.

The violet crystals turned into snow. The snowing grew heavier and within minutes the mountain range was covered again with snow.

Finally, the ever bright sun peeped out of the clouds. A small beam of sunlight entered the cave through the transparent wall of ice. "That's for you," said Grand-brother to Steve.

Steve put his right palm before the ray. A magnificent rainbow emitted from his palm and spread over the land.

Steve watched in wonder, unable to believe that he was party to that unimaginable miracle. All the birds, animals and insects came back to life. Birds started chirping, animals jumped around, and the beautiful valley was filled again with the fragrance of wild flowers.

The magical intention of love had transformed everything. Creation had won over destruction.

The group opened their eyes. They were filled with joy to see their beloved earth regain its original beauty.

"Congratulations!" said Grand-brother smiling at everyone. "See how easily nature heals itself! We've only speeded it up a bit, this time.

"And now, it's time for us to resume our journey." Grand-brother went up to the ice wall and touched it with his finger. The ice melted, paving the way for all to move out.

Grand-brother led his team toward the summit of the mountain. By the time they reached there, the sun was about to set. It cast its orange glow over the valley. Surrounded from all sides by beautiful mountains, the circular valley looked magical. The snow covering the mountain looked golden in the rays of the setting sun. As Steve stood there marveling at the beautiful sight, Cheeka nudged him and pointed toward the center of the valley.

In the centre of the valley, was a large barren circle. Nothing grew on it. Nothing seemed to even touch it. Steve couldn't even see stones within it. And although the entire region was covered with snow, there was no trace of it inside that circle.

Grand-brother saw Steve and Cheeka staring at the circle. "Yes, that is the circle of the Golden Star. See, nothing and no one can enter it. Not even snow or rain. No plant grows there. Anyone entering the circle gets pulled into the heart of the earth and never comes out. No one can walk over it. Nothing can fly over it. Such is the tremendous gravitational pull of that area."

"Only once a year, that is today, we will see the auspicious Golden Star. It will appear for just a few minutes. And that will be your chance to walk through that circle!" said Grand-brother.

The sun had set and it was getting dark. Cold winds had started blowing and the vision was not clear. Steve wondered how they would climb down the mountain. Soon night will fall and visibility will be poorer. He remembered that they had taken a whole day to climb the mountain in day light. There were just a few hours left for midnight. How would they complete their journey in time?

Reading his thoughts, Grand-brother said, "Yes, we have little time in hand. And I've not yet worked out how both of you could travel down. Our warriors are made of snow. We can easily slide down the ice. But, you..." Grand-brother stopped there.

"It's impossible to climb down this huge mountain in the dark of the night," said Cheeka, disappointed.

"Don't get disheartened so easily, brother Cheeka," said Grand-brother. "Haven't you heard that saying—quitters never win..." "And winners never quit!" Pinkoo completed the phrase proudly. "That's right, little one!" said Grand-brother with a smile. "You shall always be a winner."

Beaming with pride, Pinkoo looked expectantly at Steve and Cheeka. "We too are proud of you, Madam!" both chorused, sulking. Pinkoo cheered them up.

"Don't worry boys," said Pinkoo. "Grand-brother has helped us through worse than this! I'm sure he'll work out a way."

"Thank you, little one! As you just advised, we will make a strategy and reach our destination as soon as possible." Grand-brother looked at Steve and Cheeka, who were still frowning.

It was dark by now, and the moon had started rising behind the mountains. Grand-brother faced his soldiers and made a symbol in the air. The beautiful violet symbol lit up the place. The ice warriors understood the message in the symbol and stood in rows. They raised their hand and Grand-brother floated in the air and touched their fingers, moving from soldier to soldier. Their fingers lit up like torches. So, with their finger raised up in the air, they made two rows that moved from the top of the mountain and touched the base. Steve and his friends marveled at the sight. From where they stood, it looked like an air strip fully lit up for an airplane to land.

A small group of soldiers were waiting near the kids. Grand-brother, who was still floating in air, signaled at this group. They turned into globules, and formed a big block of ice that looked like a sledge. Then Grand-brother turned to the boys. "Your vehicle is ready, my friends." Steve looked up at him in amazement. "Yes, brother," said Grand-brother "Just step on it."

Steve and Cheeka climbed on the ice block and it started moving. Grand-brother moved ahead of the block, as it started to slide down the mountain. Traveling through the path made by the soldiers holding their lights, the block of ice caught great speed. Steve and Cheeka were thrilled. Pinkoo peeped out of his pocket and shouted, "Yippee! This is the most thrilling roller-coaster ride in the world!"

The ice sledge jumped through the ups and down, tilted and twisted at the sudden turnings and even took summersaults in the air, until they finally landed safely at the base of the mountain. The kids were dazed.

"Wow!" said Steve.

"This was unbelievable!" followed Cheeka.

"Can we do that again?" was Pinkoo's request. Everyone had a hearty laugh.

Finally, when the children recovered from their excitement, Grand-brother spoke, "Thank the Lord that we made it fast. We still have quite a bit of a distance to cover. The moon will be our guide."

A lovely full moon had spread its light all over the valley. The sky was filled with stars that looked so bright that Steve felt he could stretch his hand and catch them. Grand-brother and all the ice warriors were glowing in their violet light. Everything around was so peaceful. Surprisingly, there were no sounds around. Not a bird, not even an insect. It seemed as if no one inhabited the place. As the party moved on in silence, Steve felt a slight tremor in the ground. He thought he was imagining. A few steps ahead…another tremor.

"Stop!" said Grand-brother.

As everyone stopped and looked at each other, Steve confirmed, "Did you feel it too?"

"Yes," said Grand-brother. "We all felt the earth rumble." He looked around with his powerful violet ray. But nothing could be seen. He paused for a while and said, "This part of our journey may seem easy, but this is also the part that needs utmost caution. I urge everyone to stay together and take every step with care."

"I am scared!" said little Pinkoo, before ducking back into Steve's pocket.

"Don't worry, everything will be fine," assured

Steve, although he was himself uneasy.

"I don't like the smell of this place," said Cheeka, sniffing around. "There is something in the air."

"I can feel that too," said Steve. "But, let's just keep going. We got to reach our destination before midnight."

The party continued in silence. But this time there was uneasiness about the silence. The moon was shining brighter and things were clearer. The barren circle was getting closer.

They kept moving slowly and cautiously until they reached the spot where the snow cover ended. Steve looked straight ahead at the vast expanse of naked land ahead of him. "What a creation of God!" wondered Steve.

As the group stood there in silence, it started snowing. They had all experienced snowing before, but this was different. Snow fell and settled on the ground all around, but the snow that fell inside the circle, disappeared. The circle of the Golden Star remained stoically unaffected. "It seems so strange, Grand-brother?" asked Steve, "There is not even a spot of snow inside the circle?"

"There are certain things on this earth which can't be explained. Where logic does not work, what science cannot explain," said Grand-brother. "We have to simply accept it as a wonder created by God. A few more moments and you will witness many more amazing wonders."

Cheeka came closer to Steve and quietly held his hand. Steve knew that his friend was as apprehensive as himself. He remained close to Cheeka, as they waited silently for midnight. Gradually, the snowing slowed down and stopped. The sky cleared. Steve and his friends looked up to see the moon right on top of them. It shone brighter than ever and its beam shone straight down at the centre of the circle.

*

REACHING FOR THE STAR

"I think the time has come to welcome the Golden Star." said Grand-brother. "No matter what happens, no one will enter the circle before I say so. My brave Viola warriors, you will stand exactly around the border of the circle. The moment you see the first glimpse of the Golden Star, throw your snow strings across the circle and weave a net as fast as you can. Remember to leave a passage for Steve and his friends to go to the Golden Star." He then turned to Steve. "Listen to me carefully. Wait for my signal and don't put a single step inside the circle before I ask you to. And when I say so, run with all your strength toward the Golden Star. You can't make it out from here, but the distance to the centre of the circle is more than a mile."

"Don't forget that the Golden Star will stay for just a few minutes. Rush to it and catch it with all you got. Don't let go of it, no matter what! Remember, if you loose the Golden Star, you will never come out of this circle." Grand-brother sounded serious.

Steve listened to Grand-brother very attentively.

Although he said affirmatively, "I will do exactly as you say," he was visibly nervous.

"I am sure you will succeed," assured Grand-brother. He then concentrated on the centre of the circle. The ice warriors had queued up around the circle and were ready with their spears and ice strings to weave the net. There was pin drop silence. Everyone waited for the historic moment with bated breath. Every passing moment seemed to be very long.

Finally, it happened. First, the moon started to grow in size. Cheeka whispered, "Look at the stars!" They were also growing bigger. "The celestial bodies are coming closer to earth," explained Grand-brother.

What an awe-filling sight it was! The moon was looking like a huge, round hot air balloon and the stars like tennis balls. The whole valley was flooded with their light. And in their light, from under the earth appeared a beautiful red rose. Its petals started to bloom and the sweetest fragrance spread all over. One after the other the petals unfolded and the red rose grew bigger.

Pinkoo was completely mesmerized by the flower. "What a beautiful rose! I have never seen such a big flower!" Instinctively, the butterfly in her flew toward it, and into the 'Forbidden Circle', while Grand-brother cried in vain, "Wait, Little one…Wait!"

In an instant, Pinkoo fell on the barren ground and started to flutter.

"Pinkoo!" shouted Steve and was about to step inside the circle, when Grand-brother pulled him back. Steve helplessly watched Pinkoo tremble and loose her strength. "H…H-e..e-e-lp…" Pinkoo's faint voice reached them all.

"Wait brother!" pleaded Grand-brother with Steve…

"Just - a - few - seconds..."

And, in all its glory, out came the Golden Star!

"Now…Go…!" shouted Grand-brother, and Steve rushed toward Pinkoo, not caring about the Golden Star. He picked up little Pinkoo in his palm. She had stopped trembling.

"You crazy girl!" said Steve, lovingly. "Are you alright?"

"Y-Y-Yes…I am al…right," said Pinkoo, very weakly. "I am…s-s-sorry, Steve."

"I am just happy to see you alive, my dear!" said Steve.

Steve was putting Pinkoo in his pocket to keep her warm when he heard Cheeka screaming. "Steve! The Golden Star!"

"Run, brother…run!" shouted Grand-brother, "You have no time left!"

Steve was jolted out of his oblivion. He looked up. Straight ahead of him was the Golden Star emerging from within the earth, in all its brilliance. Without wasting a moment he ran toward it. Cheeka was close at heel. As they ran, they realized that the Golden Star was attached to something, which was emerging behind it. When they were getting closer, Steve felt that along with the star, and under it, was emerging a tree. As the tree came out, it looked familiar. He ran faster because the tree was coming out of the earth very fast and the golden star was going higher up. By the time he reached the tree, most of the tree was out of the ground. Suddenly, Steve realized what it was and stopped.

Cheeka, who was close behind him, almost bumped into him. "What happened, Steve? Why did you stop? What's wrong?"

Steve was rooted to the ground, mouth wide open, and was staring at the tree.

"Hello!" said Cheeka, loudly so that Steve would get back to his senses. "We are running against time, Steve!"

"Don't you see, Cheeka?" said Steve, still lost in the tree. "It's a Christmas Tree! It's CHRISTMAS my friend..." shouted Steve. "It's C-H-R-I-S-T-M-A-S!"

Christmas...what he had missed all these days was here! Christmas, for which he was preparing buns with the friends of the orphanage. The Holy Family orphanage, his home in New York, in his own country... America, from where he was thrown out, for no fault of his. His mind held on to the Christmas of his country that he had left behind. Everything flashed before his eyes. He had given up hope of celebrating Christmas ever after, but God blessed him with this sight. And what a glorious Christmas tree it was! The largest Christmas tree he had seen in his life...beautifully decorated with festoons and bells, which glittered like jewels. What an unexpected gift this was. With tears of joy Steve said to himself "Merry Christmas!"

"Christmas?" said Pinkoo peeping out of his pocket.

"Yes, my dear! Merry Christmas!" said Steve,

jubilantly, "MERRY CHRISTMAS, everybody!"

"Merry Christmas, my brother!" shouted Grand-brother. "We will celebrate, but right now...don't forget your mission. The Golden Star will not remain there for long. Just Go - For - It!"

Steve ran and hugged his beloved Christmas tree. He started climbing up with Cheeka right behind him. It was a huge tree and climbing it was not easy. Time was passing fast and both the boys were putting in all their efforts to keep going. They had reached half way up the tree, when a huge tremor stopped their progress. Steve held on tightly to a branch, while Cheeka clung to the trunk.

The tremor was growing and the boys could hear a huge commotion at a distance. Cheeka sniffed the air and appeared very worried. The tremor and the noise grew louder. Steve looked around to see what was happening. Running toward the 'Forbidden Circle' from all directions were hundreds of Yetis. They were advancing with war cries, all set to grab the Golden Star.

"Cheeka..." Before Steve could complete his sentence, Cheeka interjected, "I know, I know...I had recognized their scent from a distance. If they reach this tree...we're done for!"

Once again Steve had underestimated Grand-brother's foresight and the Viola tribe's commitment to the mission. Grand-brother and his brave warriors were communicating with each other in some sign language. Grand-brother made a violet symbol in the air, and in no time all the ice warriors turned into globules and merged into the snow. The Yetis kept running blindly toward the tree unaware of what was awaiting them. They ran into the circle and rushed toward the Christmas tree. Once they were all inside the circle, Grand-brother made a signal, and all the ice soldiers sprang up from the snow and pulled the net of ice strings. The very next moment, all the Yetis were down on the ground. The ice strings that appeared thin were so strong that not one of those humungous creatures could move.

"Brother Steve! You are safe. Go on!" shouted Grand-brother. Steve and Cheeka continued climbing the tree with all their strength. But they had lost a lot of time and to their great desperation, the Christmas tree had started its journey back into the earth. Their hands started slipping from the branches. Steve knew that if he lost his grip and fell on the ground, all will be lost.

"Don't give up, my friends!" shouted Grand-brother. "This is your last chance."

Both the boys made a final attempt and were about the reach the Golden Star, when a tremendous noise shook the whole mountain range.

"A-a-a-r-gh!" shouted King Yeti, as he attacked.

The booming yell gave Cheeka such a jolt that he lost his grip and fell. At the nick of the moment, Steve extended his leg, and Cheeka managed to catch it. Steve was shaken up, but somehow managed to hold on, as the Christmas tree gradually moved downward. Steve knew this was his last chance. A little slip and he would not only miss the Golden Star, but would also perish inside the 'Forbidden Circle'.

"Hold on Cheeka and don't panic!" said Steve

and pulled himself up. He was just about a yard away from the star when King Yeti jumped a mighty leap from outside the 'Forbidden Circle', crossing over all the nets, and right onto the Christmas tree.

Grand-brother and all his soldiers watched in shock, as the Yeti shook the Christmas tree with all his vengeance. Steve was tossed around like a tennis ball and would have been thrown a mile away had he not hung on tightly to that branch. He pulled himself up, against all odds, made a last attempt and finally got his hand on the Golden Star! But the star was big and he had to hold it with both his hands. With one hand holding a branch, the other hand on the star, and Cheeka hanging on to his leg, Steve felt like he was fighting a loosing battle.

The mighty King Yeti used all his strength and uprooted the Christmas tree. Steve could no longer hold on to the branch. He lost his grip and fell. But he did not let go of the Golden Star. Cheeka fell with him. Grand-brother watched him fall and rushed to save him.

As Steve was falling, he heard that almost forgotten, wondrous voice, "Ho - Ho - Ho - Ho!"

It was Santa Claus riding the air, on his sledge, driven by beautiful reindeers. Santa swiftly came down and held Steve and Cheeka as they fell down the tree. Steve blinked his eyes in disbelief. Was he dreaming?

"How can this happen?" he thought. Was he really sitting on Santa's lap? He looked at his hands and saw that the Golden Star was with him. He further tightened his grip on it, as the reindeers took off, leaving the fuming King Yeti and his pack of Yetis behind. Not wanting to give up, the King leaped up toward the sledge; but it was already beyond his reach. He fell down into the 'Forbidden Circle'.

As the Golden Star left it, the 'Forbidden Circle' came back to its original state. The gravitational power increased and the Christmas tree went back into the earth. The Yetis were also getting pulled in. They struggled, but in vain, because the Viola's net arrested them completely. They had to yield in to the power of gravity. Their King, however, had sensed the danger earlier. As the power of gravity increased, he had felt an unusually strong pull toward the earth. He had stood on a sinking Yeti and had taken a giant leap out of the 'Forbidden Circle'.

Another few leaps and King Yeti disappeared into the mountains. Within the next few moments all the Yetis, the strings and everything that was present inside the 'Forbidden Circle' disappeared. The place had a desolated look.

Grand-brother stood silently with his Viola warriors. He looked up at the sky. The moon and the stars had gone back to their original positions. There was a sense of calm pervading the atmosphere. He closed his eyes and said, "Thank you, my Lord. Take care of the kids." He stood there in silent meditation, feeling the quietness of the place. But the silence was broken by the pleasing sound of jingling bells. He opened his eyes and saw the reindeers carrying Santa's sledge coming down, toward him. With a magical trail of twinkling stars Santa Claus came down riding on his open sledge, along with a beaming Steve, Cheeka and an excited Pinkoo.

"Hey Grand-brother, we missed you!" said Pinkoo, as they came down. Steve and Cheeka appeared jubilant.

"I missed you too, little one!" said Grand-brother.

"Without your help, we would have never got to the Golden Star," said Cheeka, filled with gratitude.

"This is just the beginning," said Grand-brother, his blue jewel-like eyes twinkling at Steve. "There is still a long way to go. You have to search for all the seven sacred paintings. Always remember that you are God's chosen ones, on a mission given by him. And what's there to worry when you have his own messenger, Santa Claus with you and the Golden Star to guide you? May God and our grandmaster always be with you! So long!"

Grand-brother and all the wonderful ice warriors bid them good bye as Steve, Cheeka, and Pinkoo rode away in Santa's sledge, jingling the bells across the sky, leaving behind a trail of twinkling rainbow stars. The valley of the Golden Star reverberated with the merriest of pleasing sounds.....

"Ho - Ho - Ho - Ho!"

*